The African Robin

An Aviation Adventure

Martin Leusby

This book contains elements of fiction. Names, characters, business organisations, places and events other than those clearly in the public domain, are either the product of the author's imagination or are used fictitiously. Any resemblance to actual persons, living or dead is entirely co-incidental (for the purposes of this disclaimer).

First published March 2024 © Martin Leusby

The right of Martin Leusby to be identified as the author of this work has been asserted in accordance with the Copyright, Designs and Patents Act 1998.

All rights reserved. No part of this book may be reprinted or reproduced or utilised in any form or by electronic, mechanical or other means, now known or hereafter invented including photocopying and recording, or in any storage or retrieval system without the prior permission in writing of the author.

ISBN: 9798320476704

Front cover photo © Giorgio Varisco –
www.GolfVictorSpotting.it

About the Author

Martin Leusby is a private pilot with over 3000 hours flying experience, based in South-East England.

He has competed in sporting aviation and represented his country, and now flies on behalf of the emergency services – which is quite unusual on a private licence.

Martin has written articles for aviation magazines including such as Pilot Magazine, Flyer and AOPA, and during the pandemic penned his first novella "The Airborne Ghost". Following good reviews, he then penned a memoir of his lifetime interest in aviation and almost forty years of private flying. The book became "Pilots Progress – the Highs and Lows of a single-engine flyer".

He trusts that you will enjoy his latest adventure "The African Robin".

Pilots and Aviation enthusiasts will enjoy the technical aspects of the book, but for anyone who enjoys a thriller but may not recognise some of the aviation nomenclature or acronyms, there is a glossary included at the rear of the book.

Dawn in Mabula

Unit 58 was the highest lodge in the Mabula Game Park. The morning sun reached it before the lower plains and filtered through the nearby trees and scrub. Even at that time of day there was life around the foot of the unit. The remains of the barbeque ("braai" to the local South Africans) that had been jettisoned over the balcony the previous night had already disappeared – the overnight visiting porcupines had made sure of that, but some odours must have remained, as the warthogs were snuffling about searching for remnants.

The dawn chorus had faded some time ago, but birds were still evident. A Grey Lourie was repeating its "go-away" call and a Crested Barbet was in the nearest tree. Martin sat quietly on the veranda drinking his first tea of the day and enjoying the peace and his surroundings. It was a far cry from his frantic travelling around the world as an export director and he was so grateful that his Johannesburg distributor had introduced him to the place. An invitation to Dick's timeshare had shown him how wonderful it was, and it took no time at all (and it was extremely cheap) to purchase a couple of weeks, one in November so they could enjoy late spring when the young animals were more evident, and then one in March to enjoy the end of summer.

Although he could have tacked on his holidays to regular business trips it was nicer to travel purely for leisure, and the enormous amounts of airmiles that he had accrued over the years, meant they could enjoy his favourite Virgin B787 Dreamliner in Upper Class. Flights were all overnight, so after dinner they would recline the flat bed seats and later wake refreshed before they arrived.

Being a private pilot himself an airliner was not his favourite form of flying, but the luxury made up for that, and before leaving the terminal at O R Tambo International

(Johannesburg's main airport) he would buy a couple of South African aviation magazines, so he could get his fix of light aviation whilst out at the game park.

The hire car had been collected from Avis Preferred and they had travelled north up the N1 motorway, crossing the "concrete highway" ring road, and continuing until they reached Warmbaths, where the local Pick and Pay supermarket provisioned them for the week including sufficient alcohol for their stay, and a local restaurant provided lunch. From there it would be self-catering all week in the Unit, but it was a small price to pay (both literally for the shopping, and for the wonderful environment of the next seven days).

Once off the N1 toll road slip, the westbound R516 was still metalled, until they reached the dirt track that led to Mabula. The hire car that had started the journey in pristine condition was soon covered with the red dust that made up the track. Having passed through the security gates they reached the lodge to collect keys and book places on game drives over the next few days. Then they drove up the hills to Unit 58, all the while with eyes peeled as the animals were all around. In the hills it was mainly antelope of one type or another, but you could never be sure you wouldn't round a corner to be met by a wildebeest or even a buffalo. The bigger game would be on the plains when they went with the rangers on a drive.

Inside the unit, provisions were loaded into the fridge and freezer, and relaxation began. It wasn't long until a sundowner was in order, and Martin reflected on just how safe they were. Surrounded by high fences and rangers to keep out poachers, everyone staying there was known to the management, so it was probably the safest place in South Africa provided they didn't get in the way of a hippo or elephant. Tomorrow would be another adventure as they set out on an early morning drive to the lion enclosure – there was little danger there as the accompanying ranger would be armed with a rifle.

Who knew that the next day, flicking through a copy of SA Flyer Magazine would lead him to an adventure of a very different sort?

Well-Spotted

The morning drive was fruitful. A tunnel was used to access the lion area - with gates at either end used in the same way as locks on a canal – keeping the lions in their own area with just enough game for them to hunt and keeping any extra animals out for their own good. After the truck had searched for a considerable time Jean thought she had detected the pride and alerted the ranger and fellow game watchers. "No, it's just brown rocks" was the verdict. "Well, they've got tails" was the retort.

Sure enough, the truck had driven into a clearing and in the long grass around them was the pride. There were cubs too and knowing that the pride would be protective the ranger beat a hasty retreat, backing out into the open again. Once outside in safety, they were treated to an enormous roar from the king, just making sure they knew he was there.

After return from the lion area, the truck travellers dismounted and went their separate ways in their cars to their units. Whilst it was forbidden to drive into the bush itself (unless in a truck with a ranger), unit owners were allowed to drive between the various bush "camps" where there were collections of units. Unit 58 was at Sunset Hill, others were Bush Lodge and Modjaji, for example. The couple were used to making their own way around, spotting what they could as they navigated the allowed roads, slowly and quietly so as not to spook anything nearby.

With the hire car freewheeling slowly downhill, Jean spotted a leopard lying under a tree. The dappled sunshine almost completely disguised it. By the time Martin brought the car to rest, it was away – but at least they had seen it. Nearly all the "big five" – elephant, rhino, lion, and buffalo were evident on every trip to the park, but it had taken seven years to see the last, a leopard, in its free state. Jean would never be allowed to forget that she had said "Tiger!" when she saw it.

Satisfied, they returned to the unit for some afternoon sun and Martin perused his magazines. He had always been keen to read of aircraft for sale, as when they first went to South Africa, they seemed incredibly cheap compared to any offered in Europe. With labour being so inexpensive, nicely re-painted and re-upholstered machines were often available and being priced in rands (ZAR), the exchange rate meant they were bargains. But the dealers had realised why so many were being bought and exported and nowadays offered them in US Dollars at normal prices.

Nearly every aircraft on offer was a regular spam-can – Cessnas and Pipers abounded, with the occasional Mooney available. But in this issue of the magazine there was a Robin! Not the feathered variety, but a Robin DR400-180, the Regent model. In its native country it would be pronounced "Row-ban". Built in the Dijon-Darois region of France, it was on offer at an incredibly low price in ZAR – less than half of what it would fetch in UK.

It was surprising that there even was a Robin in South Africa, as wood and fabric aeroplanes would certainly need protecting from the harsh environment. A quick surf of the internet suggested the one on offer was one of only two in the country, and no doubt it would be a brave Afrikaner that would buy something the local engineers had never seen or worked on before. Martin's first thoughts were that just because of that lack of engineers with experience, it might be in a sorry state, and hence the low price.

But then he noticed the detail of the advertisement. Not from a dealer, as were all the others, but from an attorney. Anton de Klerk was a Johannesburg-based executor of an estate which included the aircraft and despite a stated price, was open to offers received before the end of the month. The machine could be viewed by arrangement at its base of Semple, wherever that was?

Serious Consideration

Whilst the Robin could be a basket-case, if it were flyable, and even if the fabric was such that it needed recovering and the interior refurbishing, a significant profit could still be made in Europe – and if an offer lower than the stated price were accepted it would be worth that just for the engine, provided it was in good condition and had logbooks.

First thing was to find out where it was, and his road atlas of South Africa didn't list Semple. He had no aviation maps of Africa, but fortunately he had with him his android pad loaded with SkyDemon – simply the best aviation planning and navigation tool of its day. So good in fact, that the company leader Tim Dawson had been made an OBE. To find Semple it was necessary to download the South African Chart onto SkyDemon and use the "Create Route" function of the software. Unfortunately, the airstrip at Mabula was not marked but by using the strip next door at Rooiberg he could see the direct route to Semple was 187 nautical miles – and whilst the strip at Mabula wasn't marked, the airspace where they launched their site-seeing balloons was – active every day up to 7500 feet (Mabula was approximately 4000 feet above sea level).

Semple was just south of a river that formed the border with Zimbabwe, and very close to the west was Botswana. The software informed him that it was a gravel strip of 1202m x 20m and the airfield plate (an image of the runway layout and with contact details) stated "no nearby town". It was the back of nowhere, and by road would be a long arduous drive.

But if a conversation with de Klerk about the state of the aircraft meant he would still be interested, there was a chance that he could rent something and fly there and back in a day to inspect the machine. It was easiest to use SkyDemon to calculate distances and whilst Rustenberg had a flying club and was the nearest potential departure point, cross-country by car to there would take longer than retracing his track down the N1 toll road and reaching Wonderboom Airport.

Whilst he'd flown from Rustenberg before, it was as part of the World Rally Flying Championships, in a Cessna 172 supplied by the organisers and delivered to Pilanesberg where the competition was based (with accommodation at Sun City). There had been a flying club at Rustenberg, but he hadn't seen what they offered, and knowing of the availability of other Cessna 172s at Wonderboom the latter seemed the obvious choice, and despite being further, the better roads would make it quicker to reach there. Their resident Pretoria Flying School was a good outfit, and it would be easiest if he simply went with an instructor rather than have to validate his licence again – that had been easy for the championships because there had been an overall waiver for those with an FAI sporting licence, but if he wanted to rent on his own it would be different.

Martin calculated that Wonderboom and return from there by car would total 3 hours, and the flights from Wonderboom to Semple and return would only take about 4.5 hours (even allowing for avoiding the Danger Areas to the North of Pretoria, so with it being March, a day (including twilight) would last 14 hours there would be ample time to do what was needed and make a thorough inspection.

But he was getting ahead of himself, it was time to phone the lawyer!

Telecommunication

Nowadays, South Africa has some 95% penetration of cellular coverage, and two of the four companies, Vodacom and MTN have the best coverage away from cities. Fortunately, the unit was high in the Mabula hills, so the Vodacom signal was strong enough for a decent conversation.

"Howzit?" was the answer from the Johannesburg number. Martin had been there often enough to know that this roughly interpreted as "How are you" but the questioner did not expect an answer, merely an introduction.

He explained the reason for the call, expressing his interest in the aircraft and wanting to know more - he'd need to know the age, hours flown, last maintenance and any damage history, and anything else relevant before he would know how interested he was. Anton de Klerk was not particularly helpful.

"Trouble is, I know little about it. It was owned by a *whenwe* who kept himself to himself. Despite being in a very secure environment, he was killed by raiders who broke into his *kraal,* and we were appointed as executors by the courts".

Martin knew *whenwe* meant an ex-Rhodesian. When Mugabe took over and formed Zimbabwe, farms and land were "redistributed" and the white settlers were forced out, many to South Africa and they earned the nickname by always saying "when we lived in Rhodesia" and complaining how worse off they now were.

"His *kraal* is quite a decent estate, a farmhouse that should have been secure – a well-fenced gated community holding his staff and quite a lot of land. But he had no family that we know of, so it's just a matter of getting rid of everything he owned on behalf of the government. The aircraft is in a locked hangar at Semple, and I haven't even seen it. The paperwork shows it was purchased after he moved there shortly after April 1980 when

Zimbabwe was formed, and there is something about having a previous French registration but that's most of what I know".

Disappointed, Martin explained that he'd need much more before taking the trouble to visit. Did Anton have any logbooks, or perhaps bills from maintenance companies – anything that could give more clues?

"I can look through what I have. His accounts are here so there might be something. But the big problem is that we have an offer for the estate that should complete in less than six weeks, and we want the whole thing to be finished and get paid. The hangar is rented and costing money, so if we haven't sold the aircraft by then, we might as well send it for scrap. Give me your cell number and I'll call you back".

Having done so and hung up, Martin considered again. It sounded like *any* price could be the right price, which was very tempting. Tempting enough to risk the investment of a flight up there, which would be enjoyable enough in itself. Time to speak to the Pretoria Flying School!

Aircraft Rental?

As expected, Pretoria Flying School would be happy to help. Grant, the chief flying instructor, had flown with Martin before on a previous visit, and as long as he was on board, Martin could do all the flying and Grant would be there to ensure legality and help with any local airspace quirks. Even with the cost of him being aboard, the overall hire rate was probably half of the UK rate, little more that the direct costs of fuel if Martin was flying his own 172. So even if the Robin were a basket case and it were a wasted trip, it would be an enjoyable day, flying above Africa again.

Furthermore, whilst Martin waited to hear from the attorney, Grant was happy to ask around if anyone knew the aircraft, or any local maintenance companies in or around Semple. There was no need for concern that they (the flying school) would be interested in the aircraft themselves as it was such an unknown type to them and would be unlikely to survive their outside tie-downs under the hot sun. Metal aeroplanes were much more desirable.

The conversation was left there. News was needed from the lawyer, and there was no time to waste.

Really?

The next day, Anton de Klerk came back with news. Having searched through paperwork, it was apparent that when the aircraft first came to South Africa it was maintained by a freelance engineer, Andries Venter, who eventually set up Gemair initially at Grand Central airport, but later moved the operation to Lanseria Airport and the aircraft would be flown to there for its annual checks.

Whilst Gemair looked after it for several years, they had only really had to do general servicing of the engine - which was a conventional Lycoming O-360, just like all the Pipers and Cessnas they looked after. When further maintenance on the structure was needed, it was outside their confidence, so it was recommended it go to Adventure Air who specialised in home-built aircraft and less conventional types.

The bills showed that Adventure Air had worked on the fabric of the aircraft, installing new inspection hatches to the underside of the wings, and made some remedial repairs to the undercarriage, along with subsequent annual inspections. Anton gave contact details at that organisation – either Lande Milne or Candice Chetty should be able to help – and they were at Wonderboom Airport. Result!

Candice (and Ron)

Whilst Martin's home base of Rochester was (and is) lucky enough to have a lady engineer, in the form of Carol at Arion Aviation, it is unusual. So it wasn't surprising for Candice to explain that whilst she was "front of house" at Adventure Air, she would need to check what they knew with the chief engineer and get back to Martin as soon as she could.

Good to her word, it was less than an hour before she came back. Ron Stirk, chief engineer, was put on the line and after an explanation of why the enquiry, he was saddened to learn of the owner's passing of which he had no prior knowledge. In fact, he'd been expecting to hear from the owner soon as the mandatory annual inspection was due any day. The logbooks were all kept at Wonderboom, and yes, he'd be happy to photo any significant pages and email across to Martin.

A good salesman, like most South Africans, he pointed out that if a purchase was on the cards, then an export Certificate of Airworthiness would be necessary, and he knew just the firm to do it.

Later that day a collection of pages from the logbook arrived on Martin's phone and he got his first real knowledge of the aircraft. Built in 1981 it had arrived shortly after and been placed on the South African register. In the following 30 years or so it had only accumulated nearly 2100 flying hours, and whilst the mandated TBO (Time Before Overhaul) of the engine had been exceeded, as a privately-operated aircraft it was being flown "on condition". As long as it performed well and had good compressions, the owner did not have to replace the engine. It had had a top overhaul only 200 hours or so previously and with new cylinders fitted should be good for a considerable time.

It was looking to be a good investment. Martin had already been in a good mood, which was now heightened and yet he was concerned that all this was detracting from Jean's holiday – but opportunities like this are rare and if successful it could fund several more holidays!

Darling, I need to go flying…….

This brought a reminder that it was *their* holiday, not just his, but after the explanation Jean was soon on board with the idea. She had always relied on him to make good financial decisions and it was his acumen that meant they could enjoy South Africa whenever they wanted. But agreement came with instructions, and if he was in any doubt about the aircraft then it should be forgotten immediately and simply put down as an enjoyable day's flying, and they could get back to game drives and braais. Fair but firm.

The number of subsequent phone calls would have cost a fortune in roaming charges, but with previous experience of high costs, he had bought a local sim on arrival, and would only be paying local rates.

De Klerk was first, supplying the address and telephone number of the deceased's *kraal*, where he could talk to Dale, who managed the farm, and who could meet them and supply keys to the hangar at Semple. Hopefully he would also know some more about the aircraft and how it had been used. Dale was being retained by the law firm until the estate transfer was completed and would be hoping to be taken on by any new owners, so was bound to be helpful.

A quick initial call to Dale, and it was good to hear that any day in the next three would be convenient and he just needed an hour's notice to get to the airfield at Semple and greet them.

Next it was Grant at Wonderboom to arrange the flight. Not having been expecting to fly, Martin had no headset with him, but yes, Grant could loan him one from the flying school. Any of the next few days would work for him, so it was decided to make an early start the next morning. Once at Wonderboom, Dale could be called before take-off with an ETA for their arrival.

With that arranged, it was time to study whatever he could find on the web about Robin Regent aircraft. Were there any inherent problems he should look for? What about performance, range and endurance, handling? As a Cessna owner he flew an aircraft with a control yoke, but the Robin would have a control column or "joystick". He'd flown aircraft with joysticks before – not least Chipmunks when he was an Air Cadet, but that was for short, half-hour air experience flights when he was younger and before his right shoulder was damaged in a road traffic accident. He needed to know the control layouts to see if he could fly left-handed for long periods.

He'd only ever flown one Robin before and that was a little aerobatic 2160D. He seemed to remember there were two throttle knobs - one at either side of the cockpit, unlike the central throttle of the Cessna. If he was to keep his good arm on the joystick for long periods, it might be best to fly from the right-hand seat so he could operate the throttle with his right hand.

Normally the captain would always sit on the left, and it would be a bit strange to fly from the right, but he had done it a couple of times previously when allowing very good friends to fly his own aircraft but with him alongside in case he needed to take over.

None of this would matter if the aircraft didn't look right to him, but he continued to study everything he could find, so he would be better prepared to inspect the craft.

Meanwhile, Jean refused to waste her day, and had spent the morning keeping an eye on the young calf that a waterbuck has deposited in the bush below the unit. It was as if the mother wanted it left for protection as she went foraging, and sure enough, whenever the warthogs appeared and started snuffling about and getting too close, Jean would shoo them away.

Eventually mother waterbuck returned, nuzzled her young, and as the two of them trotted away she could see the white ring of fur that encircled their tails.

Jean never strayed far from the unit on her own as you never knew what you might meet. It had even been known for hippos to walk through the camps and you should never come between a hippo and water. But the nearest waterhole was only a few yards away, and once the waterbucks had gone Jean ventured there and was greeted by the sight of a Red Bishop. Only a small bird amongst the reeds, but it was vivid scarlet – almost luminous. It was probably one of their favourites to see. Whilst game and the big five were the main object of the visit, the wonderful birds added another dimension and there was so much variety.

So much, that on arrival they had borrowed a copy of Newman's Birds of Southern Africa from the entrance lodge. It didn't help them identify LBJs (little brown jobs) but anything with colour could usually be found and noted as seen.

Unusually today, as she wasn't in the open veldt, she also spotted a lilac-breasted roller. The most beautifully coloured bird with lilac chest and blue wings (and about six more colours throughout its plumage), as it flies it rolls from side to side and hence its name. At about the same size as a magpie, they can usually be spotted on sparse trees or power cables, and about the only downside is their horribly harsh call – it simply doesn't suit such a beautiful bird!

Pleased by what she had seen, Jean returned to the unit as it was nearly time for a sundowner, and to prepare for the evening braai. Martin was still in front of his android pad, scribbling notes furiously.

But how will you get it home?

Eventually he gave up making notes and concentrated on Jean. Tonight's sundowners of choice would be bottles of Savannah dry cider with a twist of lemon squeezed into the necks.

Sat on the balcony of the unit they enjoyed the warmth of the evening, whilst the braai gained heat from its burning lumpwood – not charcoal as they would use back in UK. It would be important to be eating before the light went completely or they would be invaded by countless insects attracted by the fire and the lights of the unit. As dusk fell, the chorus of crickets commenced but was soon overcome by the sound of chicadas – just beetles but if close enough, with the sound of a chain saw.

Jean couldn't resist asking, and Martin didn't know the answer, yet. If it were a Cessna or a Piper, it would be relatively simple to unbolt the wings, push it into a container and ship it home by sea. Actually, there would be a lot more to it, protecting the aircraft from movement etc., but that wasn't relevant as the Robin was wood and fabric that was best left undisturbed.

The most obvious answer was to simply fly it home, but all the way from Johannesburg to Kent? The airlines who fly at such a height that they can route almost direct, take some eleven and a half hours to cover the 5600 miles to Heathrow. Despite some claims he had read for higher speeds, it was unlikely that he could get more than 125 knots airspeed. A direct line would probably mean some 39 hours flying and a direct line wouldn't be possible, so with a route necessary with multiple stops for fuel it was bound to take at least 50 hours.

Back in 1939, Alex Henshaw had flown a Mew Gull (G-AEXF) from Folkestone to Cape Town, arriving after just under 40 hours from when he set off – but that was in a racing aircraft that covered the 6377 miles at 209 mph. And he was a young man of 26. He had only had to land for fuel three times, touching down in Algeria, Belgian Congo and Angola.

Neither the Robin nor Martin would have that much endurance, so it would need careful planning. Not least would be the need to keep the whole flight time to less than 55 hours, as if it were to commence the trip with a new export Certificate of Airworthiness following the annual inspection, it would require a maintenance check 50 flying hours later, which he would be allowed to extend by 10% to 55 hours.

There was also the matter of permissions to fly through/over countries and it would all need investigation, but others had done it, so why couldn't he? All this was pondered as they worked through the braai and a fine local red, and then it was time for an early night as they would be up early in the morning.

No alarm clock needed

An overhead flight of a flock of Hadeda Ibis roused them just after four. Their insistent cry of haa-haa-haa-de-hah was enough to wake anyone. Usually present in the cities where they feast on massive rubbish tips, there must have been something local that was attracting them.

Dawn started to break at 05.15 and as the sun rose at 06.00, Martin was already in the shower. "Have you decided if you are coming?" he asked Jean. Much as Jean used to enjoy flying in UK, Europe and the Channel Islands, that was when they were both younger and more adventurous. Two long drives, two long flights, and hanging around whilst an aircraft was inspected didn't have great appeal.

"I'll stay here but you must promise to be extra careful, both driving and flying". He certainly would – not just for his own sake, but if anything were to happen, Jean would be left at the game park with no transport and no husband to look after her. That couldn't be countenanced.

Breakfast fruits were consumed, and it was time to set off down the hill in the Volkswagen Polo. Not a big car, but large enough for the two of them and their luggage, economic, and yet gutsy enough to cope with the altitude and hills. It was necessary to check out at the gate, where security noted his name, numberplate and expected return time. Then it was onto the dirt road to retrace his steps to the N1.

Wonderboom was just north of Pretoria so considerably closer than Johannesburg - they had stopped there on previous visits so Martin could get his fix of aviation, and that's how he knew Grant and had flown with him – long before the World Rally Championships. His estimate for driving time proved good and he reached there in less than an hour and a half despite having to regularly stop and pay tolls.

"Howzit" said Grant "Long time!". Grant had already planned the trip, having spoken to the owner of Semple, and the 172 ZS-LZH was fully fuelled and ready. It was a 172 Skyhawk 2, so sat slightly lower on its undercarriage than Martin's own Cessna, an old F172H. Only a few inches, but necessary to remember when flaring for landing.

The other difference was that the Skyhawk II held 204 litres of fuel and could therefore make the return trip without refuelling. Martin's own F172H only held 141 litres.

Once strapped in, they reviewed the flightplan. Happily, Grant used SkyDemon too, so the format was familiar. A direct route to Semple would have been 223 Nautical Miles on a magnetic heading of 036 degrees, but this would take them through the danger area just above Wonderboom, so Grant had planned a dogleg to slip between the two danger areas FAD 127 and FAD 129. They would then turn before passing above the Ditholo Helistop, and the direct track from there would almost overfly his Mabula game park and had the advantage of avoiding the Nylstroom Danger Area just east of Warmbaths. This only added about 15 miles, so the flight time should be 2 hours and 15 minutes.

Once fired up and taxying, the benefits of flying with Grant were quickly apparent. Knowledge of local procedures, airport layout, and most importantly language – all just made it easier for Martin to simply steer and fly. The borrowed headset was quite a decent, old David Clark H10-40, but it lacked the noise-cancelling electronics his current set at home had and didn't have Bluetooth either. If this trip meant he would return for the Robin, he vowed to bring his own headset to give him more chance to hear and understand the controllers and their accents.

After power and control checks, Martin lined up on Runway 29. Even at that time of the morning the day was getting quite hot, but with a runway more than a mile long there was no concern about performance issues, despite the airfield being at 4095 feet above sea level. Full power and they were off.

Enroute Scenery

Handling felt just the same as his own 172, but the engine wasn't as powerful, being 160HP rather than 180HP – but still very adequate. But it was necessary to climb as quickly as possible as minimum safety heights were 5700 and 5800 feet on the first two legs and then it would be necessary to be above 7600 feet for the long, 194 nautical mile leg.

They had turned slightly starboard to track to the Visual Reporting Point at Rosslyn and this had carried them over the suburbia of Pretoria, but on reaching another right turn took them out of the Special Rules Area and between the danger areas. They were active every day and up to 10,000 feet, so to be avoided.

The suburbs had fallen away, and the veldt was beneath them. Little of anything to see as they had climbed to safety height. But it was a clear day and soon the next turning point, the large lake at Borakalola National Park came into view. Once overhead they turned onto 045 degrees magnetic for the final leg.

It wasn't long before they were passing Mabula, but it was quite a way out to the left. Martin thought he could just make out the little airstrip below Sunset Hill but again they were climbing, to avoid the Waterberg Mountains and that was more important. The landscape became more and more rugged and despite several nature reserves shown below, it was not obvious where any accommodation was within them, if any.

They droned on, making regular checks on engine and fuel but there was virtually no-one to talk to on the radio, so they amused themselves swapping aviation experiences. Then half an hour before their due arrival at Semple, they passed close to the highest ground next to their course at 6,729 feet. That's why they needed to be so high!

Shortly after, they passed by the danger area surrounding the Venetia Mine which went up to 5000 feet and was needed to avoid blasting that went on. The enormous crater looked like a quarry, with what might have been two earlier "quarries" now filled with water nearby, and there was an airstrip just south of the enormous hole that also showed up on SkyDemon.

"What do they blast for?" Martin asked. "It's De Beers – they get 40% of all their diamond production from there" was the answer. Martin had always imagined diamonds were dug out like coal from underground shafts, but on reflection, open cast coal mining had become normal, and this was probably their equivalent. On previous visits, he had flown over mountains that were being decimated and sliced up for their marble and judging by the size of the crater, the South Africans didn't do anything by halves. What Martin was unaware of, was that the Venetia Mine could produce around seven million carats of diamonds in a year and was now commencing to tunnel as well to extend the life of the mine.

It was only another 10 minutes before they would reach Semple, and a descent was commenced as the strip was only 1670 feet above sea level. Grant had phoned Noordgrens (who were the owners of the strip and agricultural machinery suppliers) and knew there was no radio, so it was a simple matter of joining left base for Runway 28. The runway paralleled the Limpopo River which was the natural border with Zimbabwe. There were cultivated fields all around, no doubt fed from the river, and just by the threshold of 28, there was a solitary hangar. Opposite on the northern side of the runway was a dwelling, but that was all.

Remembering the difference in undercarriage height, Martin made a decent job of the landing. Not his best, but it had been a reasonably long flight in a different environment, and he was happy to land.

The runway description had been gravel, but it was well compacted, and they weren't too worried about the propellor picking up stones.

Grant was almost complimentary. "Wow! Even a blind squirrel finds a nut sometimes…" was his attempt at humour. They were really getting on quite well, and Martin had been thinking that if he needed to validate his licence for South Africa then Grant would be a good choice for the flight test. With that, they turned 180 degrees and backtracked to the hangar, where Dale was waiting and grinning at them.

Back at the Unit

With Martin dispatched, Jean had decided on a return to bed for a couple more hours, but the bush seemed noisy today and the chorus of croaking frogs (or were they toads?) kept her awake. They had put off the game drive that they had booked for today and would not do an early one tomorrow as Martin would have had a long day today, and an early rise might not be on the cards. If he could get that aeroplane out of his mind, they might manage a dusk patrol, or even a night drive.

But now the maid was due, so Jean arose and dressed. The annual levy they paid for the timeshare included any necessary maintenance on the unit (this year they had had new soft furnishings), up to ten game drives (any extra were chargeable), and a twice daily visit from the maid. She was dropped off at the unit by a truck after breakfast, did all the dishes from the morning meal and the night before, made the beds and then cleaned the unit. Then she wandered downhill to the next unit to do the same and so on. In late afternoon she would return briefly to take care of any lunchtime crockery.

Although the unit was self-catering, there really wasn't much for Jean to do except relax and enjoy the surroundings. Martin having taken the car, there was nowhere for her to go, so armed with some magazines from home, the Newman's bird book, and her Opticron field glasses she sat on the balcony, reading and listening.

At midday she was happy to receive a call on her mobile – Martin letting her know they had landed safely at Semple. Years previously she had spent several worried hours in an Orlando hotel whilst he was flying down to the Florida Keys, and it was very dark when he finally got back. It was the days before cellular phones so there was no easy communication, but since then there was new technology and she had ensured that he was trained to use it and keep her informed. Thinking about how well he now behaved brought a smile to her face as she imagined what he would be saying to Grant about how he had done his duty in calling her.

The beauty of sitting quietly, was that you can hear the game as it approaches and passes by, foraging across the hill, and if no rapid movements are made, they are happy to graze in front of you. Throughout the afternoon a succession of antelope passed by. There were the usual families of Impala with lots of young at this time of year, and then a much larger Kudu with its long, spiralled horns, enormous ears, and white-striped body. But today's rarity was a Klipspringer that appeared on the rocky outcrop at the side of the unit. Small, sweet-looking and shy, they have blunt hooves to allow them not to slip on rockery, and spring onto it as their name suggests. Only the second time in seven years for one to appear, and Jean was happy.

There were lots of LBJs too, but then a Crimson-breasted Shrike appeared. So distinctive, Jean didn't even need to look it up. The peace was then shattered by a group of Francolins, looking like pheasants without tails, their cackles as they rummaged around the base of the unit drowned out anything else she might hear.

But they were soon to move away when the first baboon of the day announced his presence with a horrible bark that received similar replies from all around. Baboons tended to arrive in troops, moving across the hillside foraging and having no fear of humans. Jean knew it was time to go inside and close windows and doors.

Within seconds they were on the roof and then jumping down to remove the apples that had been stuck on forks pushed into the wooden fence surrounding the balcony. Whilst guests were not supposed to feed any animals, a juicy apple would often attract a Barbet or other friendly bird to engage at close quarters and result in a great photo opportunity, and it was natural food anyway, so what's the harm?

The obvious answer is that it also attracts baboons who you don't want to see that close! As Jean walked into the lounge, she was startled to see a big male almost as tall as herself stood looking at her through the window. She jumped with surprise.

Once anything edible had been removed the troop moved on and their barks faded as they moved down the hill. The maid, who had been awaiting their departure, now appeared for the afternoon dishes but found nothing to do and happily left.

As dusk approached Jean set about preparing the fillet steak for tonight's braai (the exchange rate meant that a whole fillet had been bought for the cost of a pre-packed single serving at home), and once that and a salad was prepared, it made sense to open a good Shiraz and let it breathe.

Dale

"Howzit?" Dale knew instantly which one of them was Grant. Afrikaners tend to be big, and their complexions reflect their environment. Introductions made he was as interested in their intentions as Martin was in the aircraft. "I've already opened the hangar, but it's at the back behind Noordgrens' aircraft. If you can help me pull that out, we can drag Glen's out for you to see in daylight".

Mr. Noordgrens' was a serious aeroplane. A Piper Aerostar, it weighed more than twice the Cessna or Robin and would take some pulling. Martin also thought it was a pretty large aeroplane for such a short strip, but its performance must be such that it could cope. There was a motorised tug alongside it in the hangar, but Dale had no key for it, so the three of them struggled and pushed and pulled the Piper forward. With no towbar, occasional correction of direction was necessary by a heavy foot against the nosewheel. Fortunately, there were no spats to damage.

Once there was enough room behind it, the Robin was comparatively easy to bring into the sunshine, and Martin was happy to see how smart it looked. Overall white with two-tone red accents it reminded him of a Robin he regularly saw at Rochester. That was owned by an ex-airline pilot who was now an instructor and who tended to keep it at Rochester in summer and Lydd in winter to avoid being stymied by a waterlogged runway, as so often Rochester was.

"I don't know how the wings got bent!" said Dale. They were supposed to be like that, Martin knew. When he'd been studying on the web, he'd found an explanation as why they were cranked upwards or at least a debate about the reasoning. There had been a series of cranked wing designs from "Jodel". These were aircraft (originally home-built designs) by Frenchman M. Joly and his son-in-law Delemontez, hence the compound name of Jodel. Pierre Robin became involved and started producing them as production aircraft.

There are conflicting views as to why Joly and Delemontez chose the cranked wings. One holds that Delemontez wanted to hold down the wings' bending moments at the fuselage juncture by making perpendicular wing attach points. The necessary dihedral is provided farther outboard on the wing, by the "cranked-up" portions. Another explanation is more prosaic and humorous: Delemontez' workshop wasn't big enough to accommodate a full wingspan, so the outboard sections had to be installed later. Whichever the real reason, it had been a very successful series of aeroplanes, and the DR 400 (D for Delemontez and R for Robin) was one of the best.

An initial walk-round was done to inspect the aircraft and Martin could see nothing particularly wrong. What did look different to the Robins he knew was that there were not any spats covering the wheels, and the normally shrouded undercarriage legs looked a little ungainly. In UK the spats would do a good job of protecting the underside of the wings and fuselage from the copious amounts of mud on grass airfields in winter, but maybe they weren't needed in a dry Africa? But without them there could be a chance of gravel or stone chippings hitting the fabric under the wings so that would need checking.

But the aircraft sat squarely on its undercarriage and looked "right". Moving control surfaces and checking for play in hinges, he could find nothing wrong. Sliding the canopy backwards revealed what must have been recently reupholstered seats - very plush! The dashboard would take a little getting used to, with an instrument layout quite different to his Cessna. And even if all the avionics worked well, they really needed updating.

But he was grateful to see that although it did have two throttles, one was to the left of the captain's seat, and one was central to the dashboard. That meant he could fly with his good left hand on the control column and operate the throttle with his right. Maybe his memory of the 2160D was wrong – but then it had been more than twenty years ago.

All the radios had 25 kHz spacing. Since 2018 all of Europe, which included UK of course, had mandated that 8.33 kHz radios must be fitted. This was to expand the number of frequencies available to allocate. That being the case, if his bid were successful and he did fly it home, it would mean he'd have to communicate using his 8.33 kHz hand-held transceiver for the last few legs. He'd done that previously when there was a problem with his Cessna's radio enroute to the Channel Islands, so no big deal.

All the fuel tanks had quantities marked. It had the standard 110 litre main tank, with another 40 litres in each wing, and further supplementary tank of 50 litres was fitted, to give a total capacity of 240 litres. This would need managing carefully, unlike his Cessna that simply had port and starboard wing tanks that cross fed and were purely driven by gravity. And in the Cessna, there was no need to move the indicator off "both tanks" until he was above 5000 feet.

His studies on the web had given wide-ranging estimates of fuel burn, but with the same engine as his, surely it wouldn't be more than 33 litres per hour? That would give an endurance of over 7 hours – far greater than he would want to remain in the air!

Dale agreed they could start the engine, provided they manoeuvred it so that it didn't blast dust into the hangar, which they did. Following the checklist, found in the side pocket, took quite a while due to unfamiliarity with layout and controls, but eventually the engine burst into life and the two-bladed Sensenich propellor raised a mini dust storm, but away from the hangar. There was really no engine difference to his Cessna except the needs for managing fuel pump and tanks, so satisfied after power checks, he shut it down. It was his turn to grin at Dale.

Would you guys like a Bru?

Alcohol and flying don't mix, but Dale wasn't a pilot so had offered a beer (Bru pronounced brew). Apparently, he had several in his bakkie (pick-up truck), and although Grant looked as if he just might, he was the pilot in charge, so declined.

"We do need to get back to Pretoria but would like to pick your brains about the aircraft, if that's OK?" Martin continued "Do you know how often it would fly and what it was used for?". It was important to check that it wasn't a little-used hangar queen, as aircraft engines need to be used regularly to remain healthy.

"Glen – that's Mr Meyburgh – used to visit his old friends back in Harare. Not everybody left because of Mugabe – if you had a good job in the city, they needed you. I think it took him about five hours there and back and he went about once a month". That was good news. Regular running and flights long enough to keep the engine sweet. That, added to the flights for maintenance, all added up to the average hours per year in the logbooks.

Satisfied, it was time to get back to Wonderboom, but Dale offered to show them the farm. "It's all been cleaned and tidied since the raid". Maybe next time if we come to collect the aircraft, thought Martin, but he couldn't resist asking what had happened to Glen Meyburgh.

Raiders had broken through security to get into the *kraal,* tied up the owner and ransacked the place. Not finding what they were after, they had beaten him severely to get him to tell them where to look, unsuccessfully, and when disturbed by Dale's return had shot Glen and ran.

Martin wasn't too surprised, despite it having sounded quite horrific. South Africa can be a dangerous place and raiders often cross borders for theft or poaching. Some years before, one of his distributors, Ian Downey, had been shot in the leg on his own front drive near the Wanderers Stadium in Illovo. He'd been defending his wife's handbag which someone attempted to snatch as she got out of the car. Failing, they popped off a shot as they ran. Just a flesh wound, but it didn't take long for Ian to relocate to a gated community with 24-hour security. Lesson learnt.

"But they did get one of the *kaffirs*. He'd taken a cell phone, and they traced him by the signal". Dale was showing his anger, because they all knew use of *kaffir* was highly offensive to black South Africans and could lead to legal action. But it wasn't surprising for him to be so angry – he'd lost both a friend and employer, and now his job was at risk if the new owners didn't want him.

The raider was still in custody awaiting trial and the backlog for the courts meant it would be quite some time before sentencing. No doubt he'd been under real pressure to identify his fellow gang members, but the only information he gave away was as to why they expected to find something worthwhile. Rumour had it that Glen would cruise the pawn shops of any towns nearby the Venetia Mine buying up diamonds that workers had smuggled out and sold to the shops. There was no way they could sell rough stones except by that means so accepted whatever they could get – advertising was not an option! In towns like Alldays, pickings were slim for pawn shops so they would not be too fussy how they made their Rands.

If the rumour were true, there should have been a stash somewhere, but maybe the rumour was just that.

Curiosity satisfied they prepared to head back to Pretoria, but first manoeuvred the Robin, and then the Aerostar, back into the hangar. Martin made the obligatory call to Jean to say they were about to set off, and he would let her know once they landed. Duty done, it was time to strap in and fire up the Cessna.

Dale wished them well and hoped he'd still be in place if they came back for the aircraft, but if not, he was glad to have met them and hoped he was helpful. Very much so, thought Martin as he opened the throttle and rushed down Runway 28, lifting off at about the halfway point.

Enroute Chatter

Just as on the way there, there was really nobody to talk to until they would approach the Special Rules Area surrounding Pretoria. They passed the time discussing what they both thought of the Robin and whilst they agreed it was a nice aeroplane, it would be much better suited to Europe. However, if Martin needed it to be flown there and was willing to pay accordingly, Grant would be happy to help.

That sounded to Martin like a lot of extra cost. He was going to have to go back to England anyway, whilst the aircraft was prepared for an export C of A, and his flight was already booked for the end of that week as their holiday finished. But to return and remove the aircraft his flight back again to Johannesburg could be bought with some of the thousands of Virgin Miles stashed in his account, with just the taxes to be paid.

All that, of course, if de Klerk accepted his offer - whatever that was going to be. Knowing the urgency of the sale, he was optimistic about that, but that lead to a myriad of questions about logistics. Flight planning alone would be a real task, balancing both his and the aircraft endurance. Ensuring availability of fuel and gaining overflight permissions might need professional advice. A million questions.

One that Grant could answer was about the legality of flying a South African registered aircraft on a British licence. A whole plethora of documents, all certified as true and correct would have to be sent two months before arrival in South Africa. Once there, an Air Law exam would have to be taken, followed by a briefing and flight test. Once gained, the validation would be good for five years, but what good would that be? He'd be back in Europe. Too long and too expensive.

But maybe, once the Export C of A is issued, the aircraft is officially de-registered, so what applies then? All these questions were going round and round in his head whilst in the cruise southwards. Nothing should be insurmountable provided the price was right.

With that thought they neared Pretoria, and he concentrated on making a decent landing again. Grant obliged with the radio work, and they were soon safe in the Pretoria Flying School building. Obligatory phone call to Jean to let her know, then settlement for the days flying of some four and a half hours, with a generous extra sum added for Grant's help and advice. Still a bargain compared to UK costs. They exchanged personal cell numbers in case there was a next step, and then it was back to the N1 toll road to get back to Mabula before dark.

She could tell

Jean didn't need to ask how the day had gone. She could tell by his smile that it had been good. "Let's eat first and then you can tell me all about it", and in due course, he did.

There wasn't any need for debate about whether to make an offer. She could tell he was set on it already, but was concerned about how much he might risk, not just in terms of cash but whether he really intended to fly it home. "Couldn't you get someone else to take it to UK?"

Of course, but that would deny him a once in a lifetime adventure, and with their increasing years there would be less opportunity for many more in the future. "Can we still enjoy what is left of our holiday?" was Jean's next and last question of the evening. Yes, that was possible but first he'd have to do some more research, calculations and decide on an offer before calling de Klerk. They had arrived on Sunday, and it was already Thursday, with their scheduled return flight to London due on Sunday night, and they would have to vacate the unit by first thing that day, ready for the next shareholders to arrive.

"I won't have any more Shiraz – I'll rise early and do some work before calling Jo'burg. Let's get an early night". And they did, but sleep didn't come early to either of them, each with questions and worries swirling around their brains and not helped by the sounds of the bush, which seemed more intense that night.

Martin was awake before first light, and armed with the first tea of the day, he interrogated his android pad for a considerable time. By the time Jean rose, he'd decided on an offer and once breakfast was over, he called de Klerk.

Another Offer

De Klerk surprised him. Apparently, there had been some more interest shown in the Robin. It was from someone in Harare, who had asked if someone could fly it to them, so they could inspect it there. The enquirer wasn't a pilot himself but had always wanted to learn and was willing to invest in an aeroplane and instruction.

"I don't put much faith in that. If he's not a pilot, how would he know what he was looking at? So why should I go to the trouble of paying someone to go there, if he doesn't want to go to Semple? If you are still interested, make your offer!" said de Klerk.

Martin had to agree with de Klerk's thoughts. It would be a strange person who committed to such an unknown and he pointed out how it could be a complete timewaster. Better to have an immediate commitment that he would make now if the price were agreed. Martin explained what he was up against in terms of unknown costs of ferrying, permissions, legalities etc., but was still prepared to offer his now-stated sum.

It was many thousands of Rands, but with an exchange rate of over twenty ZAR to the Great British Pound, it valued the Robin at less than a third of European prices. He could almost sense a sneer in de Klerk's voice when he replied. "It doesn't really matter to me as the cash is going to the government anyway, and they already have plenty. My fee for acting as executor doesn't vary with what I get for it. As I mentioned, it would be just as easy for us to send it for scrap, but you obviously want it, so I'll make a counter proposal".

Damn. His offer had been such that he couldn't fail to get it home at a decent price, so the last thing he wanted was to be pushed upwards. He was surprised again with what de Klerk then said. "Why don't we agree on two payments, in total 50,000 Rands below what you just offered? If you like that idea, the first payment will be 100,000 into my personal account and the second, the larger balance into our company's escrow account for the government?"

The attorney was crooked! But it was South Africa after all. Even all the presidents that followed Mandela had been accused of corruption, so maybe he shouldn't be surprised, but he should be wary. "OK. We understand each other, but how can I be sure that it will all happen as it should?"

De Klerk suggested that if in doubt, his payment could be made into another escrow account. "You can even do it on the web - and when the aircraft is transferred to you and in your possession, you can release my funds".

No doubt there would be a cost to arrange the escrow account and payment, but he'd still be better off by paying about £2500 less than he had expected. More difficult was going to be to get Jean to accept they should proceed. "I think it's doable. Email me a proforma and details of your escrow account, and I'll look at setting up a web escrow. Send me your bank details on the email too".

"You'll have the email and all details by lunchtime, but my account details will be on a text to your cell phone". De Klerk was being careful. "You have until Wednesday next week to confirm everything, or we'll look to scrap it". Nothing like pressure, then. Whilst it was an opportunity he desperately wanted to take, he already disliked de Klerk, despite never having met him.

We've only got two days left!

Effectively, Jean was correct. It was nearly lunchtime on Friday and Sunday would be packing up early and travelling to the airport for the overnight flight home. Despite the pressure for them to enjoy themselves in what remained, he needed to explain the deal.

Even when he had explained how an escrow account worked – how the money was held by a third party until the purchaser was satisfied and then instructed for the money to be paid over – whilst Jean thought it sounded a safe method, she now didn't like de Klerk either. Always one for fairness, she was good at spotting crooks and took it on herself to report shoplifters if she saw them and had once even helped police by noting a suspicious car outside their neighbours' house. It was burglars who were subsequently caught and prosecuted. "I know you want to buy it, but is it right to do it like this?"

It might be helping a chancer, but it would be saving a perfectly good (as far as he knew) aeroplane from the scrapyard. Jean knew he was invested in it – not just the costs he'd incurred flying to see it, but in the whole idea of it. Finding a bargain, the adventure of flying it home, the potential profit – they were all things that ticked Martin's boxes, so it wasn't worth arguing.

But it was worth ensuring that the next few days weren't wasted. That evening they were going to the communal braai at Modjaji. There, the game wardens would lay out an enormous fire pit filled with glowing lumpwood, and the shareholders from all the different camps, Sunset Hill, Modjaji and Bush Lodge would all bring their own meat and salad (and quite a lot of alcohol) and enjoy mixing and relating what sights and experiences they have had during the week, whilst the meat grilled. It would be a very cosmopolitan affair with shareholders from all over the world (including a fair number of British).

"There will be no discussions about aeroplanes" was a concise statement, readily accepted.

Once the maid had cleared away the lunchtime dishes, Martin set off to Main Lodge. He booked an early game drive for Saturday morning and a dusk walk for the evening. They still wouldn't have used all their allotted free drives, but at least they would be doing what they came for, and it would keep him off his android pad.

The afternoon was spent at the unit watching as the world of nature walked past. Bucks of just about every sort wandered through, from Red Hartebeest to Tsessebe. Birds came and went, and some were distinctly heard but not seen. A raucous flock of Pied Babblers were somewhere behind the unit but hidden in the bush.

They were both amused when a gang of Vervet Monkeys appeared. Like the baboons they forage across the hill, but they are sweet little apes and not threatening, carrying their young against their chests.

The unit being virtually the top of the ridge of Sunset Hill, the balcony at the rear was surrounded by bush but as the landscape fell away in the distance you could see Dick's Hill (they'd once climbed it in a Land Rover) and the plain beneath it. They had a great viewpoint.

With everything coming to them, there wasn't much reason to move about, but Martin could never resist looking all around. Going to the front of the unit past their parked car, he could see the other side of the hill, and in the grassy plain at the foot of it was the Mabula Airstrip. Whenever they were staying there, Martin would check for any visitors' parked aeroplanes. He'd once flown in himself during the World Rally Championships. With the competition finished they had a free day, so he brought the Great Britain team for a game drive. Five aircraft at once was unusual and the rangers were impressed.

Nothing was on the airstrip today, so he wandered up the track to the very peak of the hill, where the tall aerial provided not just TV, radio, and cell phone signals, but a great roost for large birds of prey. Vultures are common visitors there, but today it was a Snake Eagle – smaller than the Martial Eagle but big enough and near enough to be viewed well with his binoculars.

When he returned to the unit Jean put her fingers to her lips and pointed. Just yards away was a Common Duiker stood completely still. A tiny antelope, they freeze if danger is felt. With a keen sense of smell, it had probably sensed one of them or both. Martin's movement was enough for it to flee in a ducking, zig-zag manner. "That's a first!".

Then it was time to prepare for the Modjaji braai. A selection of meat was chosen, not least some more fillet steak and some conventional sausages. No doubt many of the Afrikaners would be grilling *boerewors* – a coiled traditional sausage – but they have an extremely high meat content and were not Jean or Martin's taste. Some Savannahs were brought from the fridge – there would be ice buckets for them on arrival – and then they set off down the hill for the evening entertainment, which would include nothing to do with aeroplanes.

So as not to spoil the mood, Martin had failed to mention that he had indeed received a pro-forma invoice by email, and there was a series of numbers in a text on his phone.

Necessary bottle to throttle time

Alcohol and flying do not mix well, as when you gain altitude the alcohol becomes more effective and a relatively sober person on the ground can become inebriated with greater height. A minimum of eight hours bottle to throttle had always stood Martin in good stead.

But the braai had been a great social occasion, meeting new friends and trying different local brews. Fortunately, all the tracks back to the unit weren't public roads, so there was no risk of police presence - but slow progress was necessary to ensure no crossing wildlife were hurt. After all, it was their country, not his.

Despite the previous evening's indulgence, they both rose early for the first drive of the day. Having driven to Bush Lodge to join the truck, they and six others were driven into the veldt by Marcus, one of the young rangers. It was good to be in one of the newer trucks as the suspension coped with bumpy dirt roads so much better. The old trucks could give you backache after an hour and a half!

Most of the game is up early too, foraging before the heat of the day builds. It seemed a long while before anything was seen, but then multiple Impala appeared, strung along the track. "McDonalds!" said Marcus. He was referring to the hind markings which resemble the "Golden Arches" trademark. By the time they reached the grassy plain, the bigger antelopes were evident. The Oryx (or Hemsbok) is an elegant black and white-faced buck with long straight horns swept back and was one of Jean's favourites. There was a herd in front of them and further in the distance the enormous Ellands were grazing.

Marcus was being quizzed about Sable Antelopes. Jean and Martin had seen them from a hide next to a waterhole on a previous visit, but that was five years ago. Now it seemed there weren't any at Mabula. Apparently whilst most of the game is owned by the Mabula company, some is owned by Whole Owners – they own their units in the park outright – and they literally trade in animals. The Sables are relatively rare and with impressive ringed horns that rise vertically and curve backwards they had fetched a good price from another game park. Shame, as they were one of Martin's favourites.

The drive continued and "all the usual suspects" came into view from time to time. Despite being late summer there were elephant calves, rhino calves and when they came as a troop across the road in front of them, even the Buffalo had their orange-coloured babies in tow.

Martin thought back to a time they were in Bakubung with his distributor, Dick, and his wife Hazel. He and Jean were in Hazel's little Honda, with Dick and Hazel behind in the old XJS. A herd of elephants appeared across the road just a few yards in front of them, eating their way through the bush. Martin had made the mistake of operating the electric window downwards to get a better photograph and the big male heard it, his ears went up and he turned menacingly looking at them. When Dick later recalled the story to the rest of his family, he said that at that stage he told Hazel to say goodbye to her car. But Jean and Martin kept completely still and eventually the big bull turned away and carried on eating. Happy days.

On today's drive, passengers were just two British, and all the others were Afrikaners. The majority were sociable nice people, but on the truck that day there was an old Boer couple who made derogatory remarks when they saw local workmen repairing the roads. There was absolutely no need for the language they used, and it was a relief when they left the truck early at Modjaji. Why do people have to spoil an idyllic scene with personal prejudices? But they were very old and maybe next year they wouldn't be there……was the kindest thought Martin could have.

Once back at the unit, they decided to do a preliminary bit of packing ready for the morning departure. With lunch completed and the maid having departed after her second visit, there was time to prepare the meal for their return from the walk at dusk. It would only be the second walk they had done in seven years.

Last time they had made the mistake of going on a horse trek. Neither were riders at home, but the horses ambled along gently and took them to places that they couldn't go to by car or truck. Moreover, having four legs, they were not seen as threatening by the game, so could approach giraffes within a few feet, and even get close to rhino. By one waterhole there had been a crocodile on the bank within yards who paid them no attention. All supervised by a ranger of course.

But once the ride neared its end, the horses knew they would be fed on their return to the stable and speeded up. At first a gentle trot that could be coped with, but then they decided to gallop the last mile or so. Hanging on as best they could, Jean and Martin were bounced up and down so much that later Martin discovered just how bruised and tender his lower anatomy had become. It had stayed like that for several days, so the choice of a walk this time was an easy decision.

The walk commenced from Bush Lodge. The ranger leading the fourteen of them was Junior – well-named as he only looked about sixteen. But his enthusiasm was infectious. As they progressed, anything they saw was explained in detail including how and why chameleons change colour, the medicinal values of certain tree leaves, and how to make a bush toothbrush. Even the machinations of a dung beetle were interesting. They learnt how to tell what type of rhino had left a dung heap by observing how the shards of digested twigs had been chewed and looked at tracks in mud attempting to identify what made them.

Everyone was wearing stout shoes, and snakes were quickly identified and avoided, if necessary, but at one stage a big

Afrikaner was struck with fear. A strapping six-footer he was not concerned with tree snakes but then he saw webs across the track and all around. Lots of them. Golden Orb Spiders had created enormous webs, and he wouldn't go near them. Junior had to explain that they were almost harmless, but he wouldn't chance it and had to be lead around them, off the beaten track. Although there are poisonous spiders, the worst result is probably a bad headache – but the sheer size (particularly of the female) is disconcerting, and each web usually contains many of them.

And so it went on, until dusk came and went. An Aardwolf was filling up on termites, when they heard an ascending "tee tee tee tee teeu teeu teeu" and Junior shone his torch looking for the Pearl-spotted Owl. He found it, but also the red eyes of some Lesser Bushbabies glowing back at him. Just a glow in the dark, but they had once visited Unit 58 jumping around the balcony to Jean's delight. Again, the fruits left on forks in the railings had done their job.

Nearing the end of their circular path, porcupines scuttled across, and a Genet made a glimpsing appearance, crossing the track.

Driving back to the unit from Bush Lodge, they reflected how fascinating it had been, and how on every trip they had learnt and saw something new. But now it was time for the last braai of their holiday. As the fillet steak slowly grilled, Martin realised he hadn't thought of aeroplanes all day.

Wonderboom again

With breakfast done, the maid having washed up and beds stripped, it was time for the housekeeper to come and check the inventory. A complete list of everything in the unit, right down to the last spoon, was ticked off to make sure it would be complete for the next residents and there was no need to charge for any broken crockery or the like.

With a signed copy they could load the car and go to check out at the lodge and return the keys to the unit. A last look for animal traffic as they drove to the park gate, and then Security lifted the barrier, and they were on their way towards Johannesburg.

At Warmbaths it was necessary to top up the Volkswagen. They would need to fill it completely at the airport before returning to Avis, but that would be airport price so better take some now. Having had to leave early and with the flight not until evening, they would need to stop for lunch, and as they would pass very close to Grant's place of work, it seemed a good idea to text to see if he was around. It would be polite to let him know of progress, and besides, the pizza at his airfield was excellent.

If they reached Wonderboom before 1200 (they would do) Grant would be there but needed to take a student at lunchtime. He also texted that he had news – whatever that meant? On reaching the PFS building, Jean was introduced, and they all went for a coffee. Grant had enjoyed the visit to Semple, and it had obviously got him thinking about how he could be further help (and maybe earn something more).

Once he had been told that indeed a bid had been accepted, he smiled.

"I was going to text you with some information, but seeing as you are here…..". Grant had asked around if anyone knew about exporting aircraft and someone gave him a name. Colette van Zyl used to work for the CAA in Pretoria, and was a good source of assistance, having helped several people get the right paperwork to get aircraft abroad. There would probably be a small fee but with the saving on getting anything wrong, it would be worth it. Her previous job meant she knew all the wrinkles.

She'd be happy to help Martin by email, explaining everything, and had given Grant her details to pass on. She had quickly mentioned a couple of things to Grant, and these included the necessary Export Certificate of Airworthiness, but also a previously unknown requirement. The aircraft would need a South African Police Clearance Certificate. This would be gained following an inspection when serial numbers of airframe and engine would be checked against the original certificate of registration and against the current C of A, or the export version, and to ensure nothing was reported stolen. The certificate would be valid for six months. The same would apply to any vehicle being exported. Part of her assistance would be to identify the best places for the parts of the process to be completed.

Martin couldn't thank Grant enough for the contact. An "insider" was just what he needed. Grant had to leave to take his tyro student flying and as he left, reflected on how he'd prefer to be going to Semple again (another hint). Promising to stay in touch, Martin and Jean made their goodbyes and went for lunch.

Later, in the Virgin Lounge awaiting their flight, Martin was emailing Colette and introducing himself. Could she send him an idea of a fee for help? He outlined some of the details and suggested they might talk by Zoom sometime on Monday, as he was under pressure to do the deal by Wednesday. Email sent, "Enough" said Jean, and they settled down to some of Mr Branson's champagne.

Back in Blighty

They hadn't drunk too much champagne, although it was very tempting, but had eaten in the lounge rather than having to wait for meal service on board and lose valuable sleeping time. Although they commenced watching a film just after take-off, neither saw the end as their flat beds were too inviting. Now it was 04.55 in the morning, and they had just landed.

As soon as Martin turned off flight mode on his Pixel phone there was a plethora of emails arriving. Most were the usual junk of sales pitches from companies he'd once been in touch with who would now not leave him alone despite him "unsubscribing" frequently. But one was from Colette who would be pleased to help and mentioned a very affordable number of Rands that it would *probably* cost. It would depend on just how much work she found she had to do, but she was an aviation person and enjoyed helping so would keep it to a minimum.

Colette was happy to take a Zoom call that day, but it had to be at 17.00. With Jo'burg being two hours ahead, that meant just ten hours to get home, prepare all the information he had and work out any questions, and once the kennels were open, go and collect Louis, their West Highland Terrier.

There was some sort of industrial action going on at Border Force and the queues snaked back and forth like those at a theme park. Even the eGates had longer lines than normal, but they still saved at least an hour's waiting, and today they were working well for a change. Their biometrics were recognised quickly by the machine, and they were back in England.

Another good feature of being in Upper Class is that your luggage usually arrives first to the carousel. Which is fine if the correct carousel number is displayed on the rolling signboard. Today it did not, so it was a matter of searching until they found the correct one, and by then the bags had been there some time.

Jean could tell Martin's fuse had been shortening. "We've got them now so let's not worry". Normally he was quite placid, but he'd told her of the mail from Colette and she realised he was feeling pressured. But with bags in their possession, they could call ahead to Purple Parking to ensure their car would be brought into the car park and be waiting for them, and it was.

Another great thing about visiting South Africa is that they drive on the same side of the road as UK, so there is no necessary adjustment at either end. Despite that, Martin determined to be careful in the rush hour traffic that was building up around the M25. By the time they reached the M2 to travel east, all the traffic was going the other way, into London, so it became an easy run to home.

Planning (Phase One)

Once Martin had unloaded the car, he left to collect Louis from the kennels whilst Jean unpacked and she had nearly finished when he returned with a boisterous Westie, delighted to see his "mum". Jean knew exactly what would happen next. Martin would leave her to it and disappear into his office to get his information and thoughts together. "We are going to need another holiday", she said to herself.

By the time of the Zoom call, various scenarios had been thought through. None of these were to do with how the aircraft would reach UK as that could be worked out later, but the urgent stuff was to make it ready to leave and they needed a plan that would work, before the Wednesday deadline, so he could confirm and send the necessary funds.

He already knew where he would like the export C of A done – ideally at Adventure Air, because they not only knew the aircraft, had all the logs in their possession, and were at Wonderboom. He was sure Grant would be willing to fly up to Semple with another pilot and one of them (hopefully Grant) could fly the Robin back, whilst the other pilot or instructor could bring back their Cessna.

Rather than email back and forth, he called Ron Stirk who confirmed they could do the work for not much more than the annual that was already due. He gave a ballpark figure which was half the cost of an annual inspection in UK but pointed out that it could take up to two weeks provided there was nothing that needed correcting (he hadn't seen the aeroplane for nearly a year). If there were more work necessary, then costs would be different. Timing didn't matter to Martin, because he knew it would probably need two weeks to work out who and how it would be brought home. And if it was him, he'd need to book a one-way flight to Johannesburg.

Grant was just as happy to be asked. His fee would be just the same as the previous flight to Semple and return, Martin paying for the hire of the Cessna and an instructor he'd nominate. Grant's reward would be flying a new type of aircraft, the Robin, and getting it in his logbook. He'd deliver to the Adventure Air apron (he knew Ron) and if Martin wanted to add a small bonus, it would be appreciated. Overall, it was going to cost less than hiring a 172 in UK for three hours, so was a bargain.

Which only left the query of how to do the police inspection and paperwork and Colette would know. Jean brought sandwiches and wisely, left him to it.

He still had some time before the Zoom call, so commenced investigations of how to set up an escrow account on the web, which turned out to be relatively simple with costs that were a small percentage of the funds to be remitted. He was ready for Colette.

Most South Africans have an air of confidence and Colette was no exception. She was very matter of fact about how easily she could look after all this, and Martin's plan so far sounded good to her. Even the police inspection wouldn't be a problem as she knew who to ask – the SAPS (South African Police Service) had their Wonderboomport Police Station just 15 minutes south of the airport. They had recently gained a new lady Commander, Portia Malatjie, and they knew each other. There was of course a fee, but if one of her people visited whilst the annual was being done by Ron, then it would be easy to check all the paperwork, see engine numbers etc. and it would cost an hourly rate that was less than the UK's minimum wage.

It was agreed that Martin would let her know as soon as the aircraft reached Ron, furnish her with whatever documents were required (once he had them from de Klerk), she would deal with the CAA, and once it was done, he would transfer the necessary payments to them and her – or if she preferred, and if he were coming to collect the Robin, would bring hers in cash and with it, his thanks. Meanwhile, he would confirm everything she needed to know, send a copy of his passport etc., and confirm that the destination of the Robin would be Rochester, UK.

It was 15.30 UK time by the time they had finished, and Martin reflected on how much had changed in communication and how he could now have face to face conversations with someone 6000 miles away. But today's pressure was off – he could make the next moves tomorrow in banking hours, so it was time to take Louis for a walk and then perhaps do some more research before the previous night's travel caught up with him and forced another early night. Jean was right, they would need another holiday!

Planning (Phase 2)

Monday's first task was to set up the escrow payments. After a late start, Jean took Louis for his constitutional, whilst Martin sat at the laptop. Pads and phones are fine for information, but he always thought financial matters should be reserved to be done on computer. Whether it was actually more secure he didn't really know, but he was a creature of habit.

It gave him no pleasure at all to pay the 100,000 ZAR bribe into the account that would pay de Klerk, and he was still a little nervous about how it would work out, but nothing ventured, nothing gained. The larger balance was transferred into the escrow account for the government as detailed in the solicitor's pro-forma.

The die was cast, and he texted de Klerk to tell him it was done and with the details of the online escrow he had set up for the crook. Whilst he awaited an answer from de Klerk, he set about withdrawing some of the tax-free cash that was sitting in his pension pot, to replace the cash he'd been using from his savings account. It was always good to have a reasonable amount of ready cash available, as if anything to do with aviation goes wrong, it's usually expensive – and he would need quite a lot of funds to get the aircraft back home.

Once de Klerk had confirmed he was happy, and would tell Dale to release the aircraft, Martin called Grant and asked him to plan collection and delivery to Adventure Air at his earliest convenience. Grant would call Dale to arrange his visit to collect and then confirm when he had the aircraft safely in Wonderboom.

Ron Stirk was mailed to say what was happening and that he should expect the Robin within the next few days.

That was about all Martin could do for now until he received any paperwork that he would pass to Colette, so the next task was to consider what the route might be, and whether he was capable of flying it safely. If not, then he might have to consider a ferry pilot.

The internet is a wonderful thing and clever searching found both accounts of people who had ferried aircraft across the world, and details of companies who helped plan that sort of thing and arrange overflight permits and ensure Avgas was available at the planned stops. A well-promoted company to do this appeared to be Prepare2Go who were based in Belgium but were run by an Englishman. Another was White Rose Aviation that was UK based. Notes were made - to be revisited and investigated later if necessary.

For the next couple of days, he researched potential routes, making multiple calculations of flying time and trying to convince himself he could do it. He had to rely on SkyDemon, his flight planning software, for information as up-to-date maps of the countries he would pass over didn't seem to be available (except for airways charts, which he would need to use so that he had something printed in case he was subject to a ramp check). The only problem was that some of the countries he thought he might have to cross were not in the SkyDemon database, but he could use his portable Garmin 496 in those areas. Once in Europe it would be easy.

From what he had read, travelling up the west coast of Africa which would seem to be a more direct route to Europe, would be far too difficult. The infrastructure for aviation was better in the east. He was certain that he had lots of time to research but was struggling to find finite information of overflight permits and facilities and costs of where he might land.

He'd previously met the head of Prepare2Go, Sam Rutherford, and research suggested that he was an event organiser as much as anything. After he'd met him, Sam had been the support for his daughter and then later his son making solo around the world flights in microlight Shark aircraft. But White Rose Aviation claimed to be "the Original Overseas Flight Clearance Specialists" and had existed since the early 1980s. The appealing thing about them was their straightforward website that listed costs of overflight permits for each country, and for arranging ground handling etc. It looked very professional, and they offered an hourly rate to make a route appraisal and consultancy, and the fee would be refunded if they were contracted to help. Martin sent a tentative enquiry explaining the basics of what he wanted to do, and despite it being late in day received an almost immediate reply email stating they would be in touch.

Thursday – a day of surprises

There was an email from UPS stating they would be making a delivery between 11.28 and 12.28 that day, and asking did he need to redirect or nominate a "safe place"? He didn't and sure enough the van arrived on time and an oversize envelope was handed to Martin.

Within it he found all the documentation for the aircraft including a bill of sale created by de Klerk and countersigned by a Pretoria-based member of the Financial and Administrative Services Department of the South African Government.

Within minutes of the envelope's arrival Grant called to say that the Robin was in the safe hands of Ron Stirk (and could he transfer the necessary funds as agreed?). Of course, he could, and would add a little to the figure later that day, when he took care of banking matters and the escrow accounts. "Baie danke vir alles" meant thank you very much.

Immediately after lunch the phone rang again and this time it was Ron. He'd already started with a preliminary look over the Robin, and although he would have a lot of work to do making tests and removing inspection panels and looking for problems, he had a question. "Would you like us to put the spats back on when we've finished the inspection?". But there weren't any, thought Martin – the aircraft had looked ungainly with its naked undercarriage legs at Semple. Ron explained that they had been removed for repair at the previous annual inspection. They had suffered a lot of abrasion and chips from landing on poor surfaces and Glen Meyburgh had wanted them filled and repainted, but wanted the aircraft back before they had time to finish the work.

They had sat in pristine condition on a shelf in the workshop for nearly a year now because Glen had done his own 50-hour inspections back at Semple and not returned to Wonderboom. "If you don't want them, we can always put them on eBay" joked Ron "but no-one in Africa will want them...". But Martin certainly did. The missing mudguards were the only things he could see about the Robin that he didn't like, and they must increase its value by a couple of grand. Like Ed Hicks of Flyer Magazine, he liked a "trousered" aeroplane.

"What would it cost?" he enquired. The answer was very little as the repairs were already paid for, and whilst the aircraft was there and being inspected it would only add a few hours to the overall job. Yes please!

For the last couple of days Martin had been worrying about "how to do the next bit" almost reaching the "what have I done?" stage, but the day's events had heightened his mood considerably and he set about financial matters, followed by copying the documentation and despatching the necessary stuff to Colette.

In late afternoon, whilst strolling with Jean and Louis he realised and stated, "I own TWO aeroplanes!" "Hmmm," said Jean "you've got to get it back yet". Despite that, there was a celebration of the story so far and a bottle of fizz was later consumed.

White Rose Aviation

Mike Gray was true to his word and called Martin the following day. Based in North Yorkshire, Mike had been involved with aviation since 1977 and had set up his business as long ago as 1984. It was a very easy conversation with a man who knew everything and had done it so many times that he filled Martin with confidence.

Once he knew the requirement, the first thing Mike did was confirm that travelling up the eastern side of Africa was the only way to go. As Martin had surmised, the west would be more difficult both to get clearances and to find the necessary Avgas. Knowing the aircraft type and approximate range he could quickly rattle off a suggested route that he had used for many others, many times.

There would need to be about seven flights to reach Europe, and from there (Iraklion) Martin could make his own plans to reach home. The obvious question would be the cost, and even that wasn't too serious. Operating on his own, Mike had few overheads and would charge as per the prices on the website. There were a few slight unknowns regarding agency fees, which could change, but he'd only add a small percentage, and there would be no charge to set up handling, so the total bill would be less than £1000.

How long would obtaining clearances take? Just a few days in most cases, but for Sudan it might be a week due to security issues. It was easy for Martin to agree that he needed Mike's help, and the next stage was that Mike would email the suggested route, a list of the documents he would need from Martin, and state which countries would need a specific mention within the aircraft insurance. That would be relatively simple to arrange, as Visicover (his insurers) did everything online and a new certificate would be virtually instant.

On receipt of the proposed route, Martin would plan the flights and check distances, compare with endurance of the aircraft and himself - and if it all looked good, confirm the arrangement. There was still a lot of work to be done to create the plans, but it was something he loved doing, and with that they concluded the call.

The Route

Sure enough, Mike kept his promise and the email duly arrived. Martin's first job was to see where it would take him and consider if it were possible for him to complete. Trouble was some of the names meant very little not even suggesting which country they were in, but Mike had attached the ICAO four-letter code for each one, so they could be looked up on the net to verify where. He still didn't have any of the necessary charts he would need, so to get an idea of distance he went to his favourite software SkyDemon. The start from familiar Wonderboom (FAWB) was easy enough as he had the South African chart already loaded, but to reach Harare (FVRG) he needed to download the Zimbabwe chart. He could then see the leg distance and at nearly 500 nautical miles, it would be the longest flight he had undertaken for many years. The next leg would take him to Lilongwe (FWKI), wherever that was!

In fact, it was Malawi, so back to SkyDemon and download that airspace chart. That was better at just under 300 NM for that leg. Adding the Tanzania chart meant he could check where Dodoma (HTDO) was, and it would take another nearly 473 NM. It was obviously going to be Kenya next, and Mike had suggested either Nairobi or Lokichogio (HKLK) with a preference for the latter. Chart downloaded, it would be a long haul at 634 NM, and Martin was beginning to doubt if he could do it. But if the Robin's airspeed trued out at 130 knots, it would be 5.1 hours (in still air).

The next three legs couldn't be seen on SkyDemon as there were no charts for Sudan or Egypt, which would lead him Iraklion (LGIR) which was Crete and could be downloaded in the Greece airspace chart. Only thing to do was resort to the Garmin 496 portable GPS he had, which was loaded with Europe and Africa and by simply creating a new route and inputting all the ICAO codes he could see the straight-line distances to Khartoum (HSSK) and then Hurghada (HEGN) and on to Iraklion. Once there he could determine his own route home as he wouldn't need any clearances.

Although straight line distances were helpful, they couldn't be relied on, as Mike had explained that the overflight clearances were from country to country and to keep costs down it was necessary not to overfly any countries that you didn't have to. Most of the tracks on SkyDemon so far were straight, but he had had to "rubber-band" the leg from Dodoma to Lokichogio to avoid going into Ugandan airspace.

An edition of the "Readers Digest Illustrated Atlas of the World" was brought into play, and he could work out that from Lokichogio he would need to arc around Ethiopia (not by much) to reach Khartoum. The atlas didn't show any airport at Hurghada, but he'd had the book for at least 20 years and maybe the airport was more recent. It was a straight line from Khartoum, as was the next to Iraklion.

Although SkyDemon didn't show any content for the northeast African countries it did show outlines of them, so he could plot a direct course from Lokichogio to Iraklion and then by using the country outlines he could drag the route to just west of the westernmost tip of Ethiopia and then pull it out to Hurghada which was easy to position as it was on the west bank of the Red Sea just below the spilt into the Gulf of Suez and the Gulf of Aqaba. From there the straight line to Iraklion was good, but half the leg would be across the Mediterranean Sea.

Despite not having the necessary airways charts (they would arrive in a few days), he had the plan to get to Europe!

Looking at the Distances

Martin's biggest worry was not just matching endurance of the aircraft to the legs, but also his own. He'd undertaken some long flights in his youth, such as Wellesbourne Mountford to Herning (Denmark) but that was the point – he had been young! So, it was necessary to print out the SkyDemon Pilot Log and examine distances. Although this would have leg times calculated with current winds they could be discarded, and the distances used to put into a spreadsheet to calculate the times in still air, and estimate the fuel required. Once in Europe he could use shorter legs if necessary and relax a little, but the numbers to reach there were all-important.

The longest leg was Lokichogio to Khartoum at 704 NM, with Khartoum to Hurghada a close second at 699 NM. In still air they would take 5.6 hours each and burn some 185 litres of fuel. With all tanks full, capacity of the Robin was 240 litres, so only an extra 1.6 hours would take it to zero fuel. Headwinds might cause serious problems, and he'd need to talk to Mike again about possible diversions.

But the main problem he perceived was his own endurance. Sure, he could fly for six hours, but he'd need toilet facilities. As he'd got older, he'd needed a bathroom more often and sometimes felt a really urgent need. There was nothing worse than "the kidney-warning light" coming on whilst airborne. He had seen his doctor about it and had his prostrate checked and all was good. The medic prescribed a tiny tablet (Tolterodine tartrate) that he tried and whilst it prevented an urgent need, it dried him up too completely and a very dry mouth ensued. Not good when needing to communicate clearly.

He'd heard about glider pilots who stayed up for ridiculously long times so the obvious thing to do was ask the net how they did it. Amazingly he found a Powerpoint presentation put out by SOSA Gliding Club (of Hamilton, Canada) entitled

"Airborne Urination Management for Pilots" which suggested lots of alternative methods, but really recommended the use of a condom catheter connected by a tube to a urine collection bag. For really long flights, when the bag was full you could seal it and fit another empty one. It would all have to be purchased and tested but it gave Martin the confidence he needed to confirm to Mike that he would want his services.

During the subsequent call he checked about payments for fuel and services at the proposed stops. Would he need cash and if so, what currencies? Mike's advice was simple enough as most of the stops were pukka airports and would accept most of the usual credit cards, so he should take his Amex, Mastercard and his own bank card to have alternatives, but also a large amount of US Dollars. The Dollars could be used if for some reason the cards were rejected, or if he had to make an unscheduled stop somewhere, as nearly everywhere would accept the American currency. "Don't forget to tell all your card providers which countries you will be visiting and give them an inflated figure of what you might spend – that way they shouldn't reject any payments, which could be embarrassing!".

And yes, Mike agreed to suggest some intermediate stops that should have Avgas in an emergency, but not having arranged handling etc. for them, they should only be used if absolutely essential. Martin would inform him when he had his outward flight to Johannesburg booked, so he could swing into action with the clearances. No point in doing too soon in case there were delays with the export C of A, or anything else for that matter.

After thanking Mike for more help and promising to be in touch, the spreadsheet came out again to look at fuel quantities and potential costs. The maximum fuel top-up per day should be around 200 litres, and each day would end with an airport hotel stay, so he would tell each and all his card issuers that he shouldn't spend more than £1000 per day in each country and that way he would be covered whichever card was accepted. On a similar note, it would make sense to have at least $3000 cash and any unused could be exchanged back later at a slight loss.

To get to Europe (Iraklion) would use just over 1000 litres in still air, and then probably another 400/500 litres to reach UK, so it was a good job that he had achieved such a good price for the Robin, but it was important that nothing went wrong to add to his costs. There was still so much to do that although he wanted to collect his new toy as soon as possible, it was likely that the two weeks mooted for the export C of A would not be enough for him to be ready.

A need to get out of the office

By now it was Saturday and there was still a tremendous amount to research, not least hotels, and then the route across Europe, but it had been non-stop on computer and phone, and he felt the need to escape. It came to mind that it was nearly three weeks since he flew his Cessna and that would be just what he needed.

Whereas many private pilots simply fly locally for pleasure, for some years he had been a volunteer with Air Search (and later the police) and before leaving for his holiday had been in the middle of a task jointly for Border Force and the Counterterrorism unit. Both had lists of airfields (both proper airports and small private airstrips) they knew of across the county of Kent, but they needed updating as new strips had appeared and old ones might have closed. Air Search had done a previous survey back in 2015, but already knew of several changes.

Martin was the lead contact for the police and had been asked to meet with a UK Home Office representative (who was really Border Force but having had some bad rep recently had re-branded as Home Office!). At the meeting he explained what Air Search were capable of, and it was agreed they would work together on a new database and link with the CT information to create one county-wide survey identifying everywhere an aircraft of any size could land and put it in the required format that would suit both organisations.

Ron Armitage had been the full-time training officer for Air Search and the organiser of the previous survey, so was tasked with drawing both databases together, and sharing out the target venues to other Air Search pilots to go and photograph. The format required was one close-up photograph of each landing field taken from each of the four compass points and a further photograph showing its location in the surrounding area. This meant a result of five photographs per site, but it would probably mean taking fifty per site and then whittling down to the best, most accurately orientated pictures. All views had to be in landscape format.

The positions of each site would be noted in various formats, not just latitude and longitude, but grid reference and even What3Words (the latter being the usual format for police). Remarkably there were nearly sixty sites to cover and that was after omitting the helipads that had previously been included. There really wasn't much point in including them as any ne'er-do-well in a helicopter could land it just about anywhere.

Martin had already completed ten sites before his holiday and had another six planned and ready to do. It was necessary to plan carefully as some were hard to spot initially so it helped to research by any possible means - which might be flight guides (only the major ones would be included) or using any information provided by BF or CT such as What3Words and then using the latter to convert to latitude and longitude to feed into GPS. Another cross-check would be to use Google Earth Pro to examine each site and by using the time-scale button you could see the history of the airstrip – when it appeared and if it was still there when the latest satellite pass was made. The size of the strip could be measured too, and its orientation noted.

Scraping all the information together meant easy planning into SkyDemon and a smooth arrival at each site with little time wasted trying to find it, and already knowing what it should look like make spotting the strips easy. The Cessna was ideal for the job, as the high wing allowed easy downward photography and another Air Search pilot, Bob Bailey, would do the camera work whilst Martin flew, as he had done on the last two missions.

Weather was important and for once sunshine would not be appreciated. At this time of year, the sun never got very high so shooting from each compass point meant that the northern shots at least could be into sun and suffer from glare on windows.

Fortunately, today was overcast but clear so Bob was duly phoned and was available, and they agreed to meet at Rochester Airport at 1200.

Once they met, it was down to business and Martin had decided he wouldn't mention the other adventure he was planning for several reasons. Mainly because it would mean long explanations and they would never get the job done, but also because if it never materialised there would be a great deal of egg on his face, and the banter from his colleagues would be interminable.

Whilst warming the engine, it was obvious that the starboard tank fuel gauge was playing up again. It was registering only a quarter of a tank, but both tanks were full and as they cross-fed, the port tank indicator showed the real situation. He always flew on time since last refuel anyway as no fuel gauge can be relied on completely. Bob was reassured by his explanation, and they went and committed aviation.

On return from the photographic mission, it was decided that Bob could now do the painstaking work of assessing all the photos, checking orientations for the required views and enhancing the pictures as necessary. Martin had done the last two sessions and had other things he needed to do.

Checklist preparation

Whilst waiting for news from Ron Stirk, Martin started to prepare the documentation he would need to carry. He might be subject to inspections in Africa (hopefully not as he would have clearances and agents/handling arranged), but once he reached Europe it was possibly (or maybe likely?) that he would be ramp-checked. He downloaded the Ramp Inspection Checklist (SAFA) and was amazed at how many things could be checked – a total of 53 items were on the list.

It was designed to apply to commercial carriers, but whilst items such as escape slides, oxygen and crew rest areas obviously didn't apply to a small General Aviation aircraft, nearly everything else could be and it included mounds of paperwork that he had to have right. The sensible thing was to create an indexed folder into which the items could be seen in an orderly manner – and with a copy of the checklist in the front, any "inspector" should appreciate he'd done his homework and possibly take some of it as read. Anything to lessen risk of delays or worse.

This alone was a couple of days work, because as every line was worked through more jobs were found, such as ensuring the latest database was loaded into the GPS and checking expiry dates on his PLB (Personal Locator Beacon) battery and life jacket. Whilst he had some aircraft documents already, Ron Stirk would supply the balance when he collected the aircraft. It was necessary to call Ron to ensure that the aircraft had a recent weight and balance schedule – he would need to include calculations and include in the folder, particularly for Europe as since Brexit, this was something other pilots had been taken to task about in several countries.

He also needed to purchase a new journey logbook, which he would fill in as he went (it was item A21 on the list), and so it went on….

As a break from the folder, he started thinking about how to get to Johannesburg. The overnight flights were Virgin VS449, leaving Heathrow at 22.30 and arriving at Tambo at 10.25. Whilst he loved the Boeing 787 Dreamliner, in economy the widest row of seats was three across, whereas when they used Boeing 747s the middle row was four across and it was worth gambling on whether you might get an empty row and be able to spread out. He had a lot to do the day he would arrive so couldn't risk not getting a good sleep, so it had to be Upper Class at three times the Virgin Points and similarly extra passenger duty taxes. The taxes were equivalent to the cost of buying an economy seat, so it was still a decent proposition, and he would arrive refreshed.

It was only four days since the Robin had reached Adventure Air (and Ron), so even if he was prepared, the aircraft was unlikely to be ready for another ten days at least, but it made sense to check flight availability as reward flights can be scarce. Sure enough, there were few available with one just twelve days away and then the next would be almost a month later.

"Ron, how's it going?" he asked, and then explained his dilemma. In the usual South African manner, Ron was relaxed and explained it wasn't only going well but had even had the Police Inspection from Portia's people and he had their necessary paperwork. It was unlikely to take another ten days to complete everything else as the CAA office was on his doorstep and he could see them personally if necessary.

"I'd just book your flight. If we are a day or two later, it will still be OK and if it's three then you can stay over and buy me a beer!" And why not, thought Martin – after all he didn't need to book a return flight, but he did need to be sure of getting there at a decent price. "It'll be a week on Thursday that I arrive, would that be OK to meet up? I won't leave until Friday as I'll have to check everything and file flight plans and so on". It was agreed that a Thursday night beer would be in order, and immediately the call was finished the flight was booked before anyone else could snatch it.

Next was a call to Mike Gray to confirm the date and start the work on permits and clearances, and with that, he'd had enough for the day and finally gave Jean some of the attention that she deserved.

Learning about the Robin

Whilst in theory he was qualified to fly the Robin it would be significantly different from his usual mount, so Martin deemed it best to get some instruction. Besides that, he needed access to a Pilots Operating Handbook to familiarise himself with the differences he would encounter and fortunately found one on the internet that he could download – it would need checking against the one that came with the South African Robin as they would no doubt vary from model to model, but most features and procedures for all DR400/180s should be the same.

Luckily, Rochester was home to several Robins. Indeed, there was one parked on either side of his Cessna in the new hangar they were lucky enough to be in. High wing and low wing types were alternated to fit the maximum number of aircraft into the space. Nearest the door was a brightly painted specimen owned by Charles Prior, who was almost guaranteed to be at the airport most days. A quick call and yes, he'd be there and happy to show Martin the aircraft.

Before sitting in the aircraft, they made a walk around it and the first noticeable thing was that it didn't have the supplementary fuel tank so it could only carry a total of 190 litres. That wouldn't have worked for the proposed legs in Africa but didn't matter for this necessary familiarisation. The flaps had to be fully down to enter the aircraft and unlike his Cessna (which was a simple step up to cockpit) he needed to climb on the wing and then stand on the seat before he lowered himself down. Not for the first time he wished he was younger and more agile.

The overall feel of the instrument panel was that it was more complex than his own, but it was 31 years newer than the Cessna, so refinements had no doubt been added. The top row of the dashboard had an array of warning lights and multiple switches for both internal instrument and radio lights, and external landing, taxi, strobes, and navigation lights and even the pitot heat was a switch rather than a pull-out knob.

The flight instruments were roughly where he was used to them, except the rev counter was near his knees rather than next to the radio stack. Most of the gauges he was used to being far to the right were alongside or under the rev counter, and of course there were more fuel gauges than he was used to. Even the heating system (which was to the far right) was more sophisticated with a choice of three knobs for demist, front heat and rear heat. It was a long way to the right, and with his gammy shoulder it would be a stretch, but hopefully he shouldn't need any of them in Africa.

On a console between the seats was the starter and mixture control and importantly the fuel tank switches. Charles showed how you could select left, right or reserve tank but also if you switched too far you could turn off the fuel completely – definitely not recommended. The fuel pump, just below the right-hand throttle was to be kept on until at cruise altitude. The trimmer sat below the fuel cock and was a simple wheel as in the Cessna.

Before buying the Robin G-ETIV Charles had also owned a 172 G-RARB (called "Rhubarb" of course), and he knew the differences he would need to explain. A surprising one was settings for the flaps. Set 15 degrees for take-off and a full 60 degrees for landing, versus nil for take-off and a maximum 40 degrees for landing on the Cessna. The flap handle was a handbrake-type lever that could well take a lot of pulling going to 60 degrees, unlike the fingertip operation of the Cessna's electric switch!

Charles confirmed that he flew it the way Martin had thought would be best – left hand on control column and right hand to use the throttle. Martin was pleased by this and when Charles confirmed that speeds of 138 knots were possible and with only a 33 litres per hour fuel burn, he was even happier and duly thanked Charles for his "tour".

Embarrassing Moments

By the time he was home the postman had been. Apart from the usual junk mail and the regular bills, there was also the "measurement guide for male external catheters" he had ordered. It was necessary to ensure the equipment was the right size so as not to risk leaks. The kit basically measured the girth of the flaccid penis – and ranged from small at 23mm to large at 40mm. Our hero was again saddened that he wasn't a younger man, and immediately ordered what he hoped was the relevant size, and one even smaller in case he was being optimistic.

The next day a courier delivery brought both condoms, tube and two collection bags to be tried and tested so that if any doubts he could think of something else. Subsequent tests were successful but left Jean helpless with laughter when she saw the apparatus.

Much less embarrassing was the arrival of multiple airways charts which were poured over quickly to confirm the routing and any navigation beacons that might be available. GPS and SkyDemon were ultra-reliable, but anything could fail and if there were VORs to fall back on, so much the better. Not having an opportunity to test it, he could only hope the King KX155 nav/com fitted to the Robin was functional for VOR use. If not, he'd have to rely on his Yaesu handheld transceiver that also had that function.

SkyDemon would warn him if there were new charts available for the countries he had programmed in, but he needed to go to Garmin to check if he had the latest database and sure enough, he didn't as they were updated every month. He would only normally update if there were significant changes to UK airspace, and the last time he did it was when the new airspace around Farnborough was created. The newest version would be available in just two days, so the necessary spend of £50 would be made then and went into the diary. It was fortunate that

Europe/Eastern Europe and Middle/East Africa were bundled together as the Atlantic International Aviation Cycle – or it could have cost even more.

Another email from Mike Gray arrived with alternate (if absolutely necessary) fuel stops, and he'd attached scans of the airport approach plates. There was no way Martin could predict weather or any other reasons for potential delays, so he couldn't book hotels for each overnight stop, and would take his chances on arrival, but it made sense to check which was the nearest hotel at each stop and add the information to his ever-growing files.

He knew that he'd have at least one night at Wonderboom, so booked the Platinum Airport Lodge for the Sunday night, right on the airport. A one-way hire car wasn't available, but the hotel would oblige by sending a car and driver to collect him from O R Tambo, Johannesburg International. Much safer than taking just any taxi waiting at the airport, and actually cheaper. Flight arrival time was given, and the driver (holding a sign showing his name) would be waiting outside immigration.

Jean, in her inimitable way, had asked what clothing he'd need and for how long and was already assembling the contents of his small carry-on suitcase. If things went well, he would reach Europe after six days flying, as he really didn't want to stop in Harare and would push on to Lilongwe after refuelling. For some reason he felt Zimbabwe, for a novice traveller there, could be even more dangerous than South Africa.

At worst, once Crete was reached, it could only be another three days to home unless the European weather would not play ball. Luggage weight would be important so there would only be one spare pair of jeans, and shirts would be worn until they shouldn't be, and hopefully there could be some express overnight laundry at the hotels.

Back-up power packs for his phone (which would run SkyDemon) were charged up and an extra one was bought from eBay, just in case it was needed, as there were going to be long airborne legs! A mount that would attach the phone was included in the carry-on, as were all the charts and paperwork, and not least his DC-1X Bluetooth headset.

Although not keen on fancy dress, his Air Search uniform shirt was included as the gold-braided epaulettes might help passage through the airports, as would his AOPA Air Crew card attached to a lanyard.

Getting Nervous

Despite being kept busy studying and restudying the route, trying to get an idea of weather for the next ten days, and ensuring enough dollars in cash were available, time seemed to go into slow motion, and he wished his Wednesday night flight was sooner. Rather than waste what time he had, it made sense to learn more about the countries he would traverse, in case any obvious tips were available re landscapes and people, average temperatures etc.

But it was also important to keep Jean on board and they spent as much time together as possible, whether walking Louis or treating themselves to lunch somewhere locally. Except when on holiday – or when Martin was flying – they were really homebirds, so it was nice to go out and be fed by someone else. Outside their domestic environment, it was easy to talk about what was to come hopefully, and they also covered what hopefully wouldn't come – both admitted to some trepidation.

As expected, Martin received instructions about how he must keep in touch at every stage of the journey, and if his mobile wouldn't work in any areas, he was to find Wi-Fi and email. Jean was given a list of the places where he expected to land and when. He also gave Jean contact details of Mike Gray, who would know where and when he was expected to be (within reason) in case she just didn't hear anything. Mike knew his way around and had contacts in all the places he was supposed to be – moreover, he was reliable and a nice chap.

Both Jean and Martin admitted their nervousness, despite confidence in each other's capabilities, and when Wednesday finally arrived, it was a relief for Martin to head to Heathrow, to start his adventure. Less so for Jean as all she could do was wait for contact and updates and would have to occupy herself looking after Louis.

Eventually, it was Wednesday

Jean was to drive him to Heathrow, as he would be returning to Rochester so couldn't take himself, and the drive would give them a little more time together before he started his adventure. There was little room for luggage in her Mercedes SLC, but he was travelling light so there wasn't any point in taking the larger Jaguar XE.

Despite the economy of not having to hire a one-way shuttle to the airport, they knew they would be charged £5 just to enter the drop-off zone there – whatever happened to flying being pleasurable? Having said that, the flight itself would be good in Upper Class and he'd eat in the lounge as usual to give extra sleeping time on board. There were only three seats to avoid in his cabin on the 787 Dreamliner – two without windows and one too near the bar and having consulted with www.seatguru.com he'd booked a port side window seat as that would not be overlooked by the centre row - as they faced starboard.

At least by going overnight on Wednesday, the drive to the airport around the M25 was quiet by comparison to when he took early morning flights whilst working. They reached the drop-off zone, and after insisting to each other that they must fly and drive safely, respectively, Martin took his single carry-on suitcase and his laptop bag and disappeared into the terminal.

This time, it was Jean who had been instructed to phone him when she reached home safely, which she later did, whilst he was still in the lounge.

Thursday 6 April 2023 - Johannesburg Arrival

He hadn't slept as well as he expected. Too many thoughts about what was to come, both excitement about the imminent journey, and some worries about the length of individual legs. Whilst he enjoyed flying solo, these would be long stretches and he'd have to be on top form whilst flying an aircraft new to him. All providing that Ron Stirk had finished on time and not found any discrepancies/faults at the last minute.

Rather than accept breakfast he tried to sleep some more but was still awake as they landed and began the overlong taxi to the terminal. The last twenty years of development had seen JNB grow enormously and constantly improve but as mentioned, with longer taxi times and definitely longer walks through the terminals.

Once through immigration, with a visa allowing a three-month stay stamped into his passport, he reflected that the departure stamp would be from Wonderboom where they had customs facilities and might be only twenty-four hours later. It would be a first to have non-complementary in and out stamps. As he made his way through the glass doors at the end of the hall, he scanned the waiting crowd, declining all the offers from self-appointed porters to take his suitcase (and earn an appropriate tip) as he knew how the system worked. Finally, he spotted his name on a piece of card being held aloft and William introduced himself and took the carry-on, leading him to the car park.

As they drove to the hotel, Martin switched the sim in his phone – there was still credit on the one he'd bought for his Mabula visit. Although he was two hours ahead of London, he knew Jean would be up and made the mandatory call to confirm safe arrival – and was instructed to call again once the hotel was reached and his room had been seen!

Once checked in at the Platinum Lodge, he confirmed he was there and the room was acceptable but not as "Platinum" as the name suggested, but hopefully it would only be for one night, and besides, that evening he would be having a beer with Ron Stirk - if everything had gone to plan.

Sure enough, a call to Ron brought him round to the hotel to collect Martin to take him to the workshop and inspect both the readied aircraft and the assembled paperwork. The aircraft looked superb! Now "trousered", the refitted spats had changed the whole feel about it, hiding the ugly undercarriage legs and it now looked like every Robin should. Even the paintwork looked far better than he remembered, and he was happy to hear that nothing untoward had been found in the inspection and everything including the SA Police permit was signed up.

Although he needed to do a mountain of paperwork including flight plans for the next day it was sensible to ask Grant his "flying instructor" to come across and to fly a check-flight with him. It would again acquaint him with Wonderboom procedures, and he'd have back-up as he mastered flying the Robin. By mid-afternoon, after a local flight, he was satisfied that he could handle the Robin and was impressed with its turn of speed. Same engine as his Cessna but the lighter wood and fabric gave an advantage, as probably did the unusual, cranked wing.

On their return, they fuelled the aircraft to full tanks, and he settled up with Grant, received his thanks and good wishes for the trip home, and then said goodbye as Grant had students to look after, and Martin had some more serious settling-up to do with Ron.

Ron had already paid Portia from the South African Police Service for her necessary documentation, and he had the bill from Colette for the export paperwork and would pass on the fee on Martin's behalf. When everything was added together, the final bill in ZAR was still only equivalent to about half the cost of an annual inspection, were it done in Blighty.

After settlement, Ron drove Martin back to the hotel so he could commence his flight planning, and he would later return in early evening for the promised beer!

Friday 7 April 2023 - Morning

It hadn't been a late night. The desire to be mentally sharp in the morning meant it had been a very quick beer, and with flight plans filed the previous day, it was an early start with a taxi around to the customs building, and once papers and passport were stamped it was over to the Pretoria Flying School where the Robin was parked.

The best thing about today's flight was to be that half of it would be the same route he had taken to Semple to check out the aircraft, so although a not very familiar aircraft, the first two hours would be a proven route, and then as he passed overhead Semple he would be entering Zimbabwe airspace almost immediately.

Once the small amount of luggage was loaded and the various bits of kit (SkyEcho2, Pixel phone with SkyDemon, GPS, and Bluetooth headset) were installed and tested, it was a call to Wonderboom Tower on 118.350 for engine start. The wind even favoured the same runway as the last flight, so after power checks, he was soon rolling down runway 29, shortly to turn to avoid the danger areas. Twelve minutes later he was in open airspace and the Robin was giving 130 knots True Air Speed, but a slight headwind element mean ground speed was 124 knots. His FREDA checks reminded him to change tanks.

Bang on the two-hour mark he was overhead the gravel strip at Semple, and seconds later crossing the river into Zimbabwe. "Border Crossing" was reported to Harare Information on 125.100 and he was pleased that flight plan details had all reached them, and he was cleared via overhead Masvingo (FVMV). Minimum Safety Altitude for the whole route was never below 5700 feet, and he cruised the whole way at Flight Level 70 to comply with the Semi-Circular Rule. Shortly after Semple, winds had become neutral and an hour later the

Southern Tradewind kicked in, and he was at 143 knots ground speed.

Harare (FVRG) used to be called Salisbury Airport, which to him sounded much friendlier than Robert Mugabe International, but the approach controller was helpful, informing of a 10-knot wind straight across Runway 05. Martin was glad it wasn't stronger as he had absolutely no crosswind experience in the Robin, and whilst he would use wing-down method in the Cessna, would have less clearance to do so in a low wing aircraft.

It wasn't the best arrival. A crabbed approach and being unused to a control column rather than his familiar yoke, saw to that. Runway 05 was a mere three miles long, so he'd had plenty of time to sort it out. Anyway, he was down, and the aircraft could be used again!

Having landed long it was a short taxi and then a left turn onto the General Aviation area which was alongside the Zimra State Warehouse. A truck soon arrived with uniformed officials, distinctly military looking, and wearing sidearms. But they were pleasant enough, and Martin wondered if his greater number of epaulette bars had helped. Escorted to customs, he explained there was no need for immigration as he would be departing almost immediately for Malawi and would remain airside. Despite that he was relieved of 55 USD, the standard fee, and which would probably never reach the authorities.

The "Corner Café" was airside, so he grabbed a sandwich and tea whilst waiting for the bowser to refuel him and sent a text to home informing where he was. Once refreshed he went back to the office to settle fuel and fees. The 130 litres were as expensive as expected but they accepted his Mastercard, and he was glad to have lots of dollars as although the landing fee ($15) and parking ($5) were reasonable, there was a departure fee of

$35, and an "airside bussing" fee of $30 each way. So - the equivalent of a hundred quid for just over a one hour stay.

Friday Afternoon

He was already tired. Not so much physical effort, but the stress of new aircraft, environment and unknown receptions had taken its toll. But there was no choice, he was going to Lilongwe – flight plans had been filed and there was just something about Zimbabwe he didn't like.

It was going to be less than a two and a half-hour flight which would be almost a direct line, with just a slight kink to overfly Songo Airport (FQSG). The terrain was still high and uninviting, so it was best to route overhead potential landing sites that could be used if necessary. Mike Gray had organised the flight clearance over Mozambique, which he would cross in their Beira Flight Information Region, and he would be overhead Mozambique for 140NM.

With all this programmed into SkyDemon and the GPS, he listened to the Harare ATIS then called for start on the tower frequency of 118.100. Runway 05 was still in use and checks done, he took the taxiway to the southwest, but the first holding point gave him a good mile to take off, and having told the tower it was enough he was allowed to go from there.

He'd just been cleared to take off when the controller radioed "We've had a call from someone who wants to talk to you about your aircraft – but we've said you are already departing". What on earth was that about? "Sorry, rolling already!" "Roger".

Hopefully it wasn't a South African official who had discovered de Klerk's crookedness and wanted redress, but whoever it was, Martin was committed to reach Lilongwe that day, and the faster he could put both South Africa and particularly Zimbabwe behind him, the happier he would be.

The minimum safety altitude was the same - so it was up to Flight Level 70 again. As he climbed outside the Harare ATZ before he left Zimbabwe, he passed overhead the airstrip at

Umfurudzi. It was an unfriendly looking gravel strip running east-west at 2625 feet AMSL and almost 900m long – so would have been helpful if there were any problems (and help would have been available from the nearby game park that it serviced).

Less than an hour later he was speaking to Beira Information on 127.900 as he crossed into Mozambique and as he did so, the ground dropped away by 2000 feet to reveal green plains below him. There was also the biggest reservoir he'd ever seen which ran from east to west and almost reached Songo. The Zambesi River runs into the Cahora Bassa Lake (he would learn later) which has capacity for 56 cubic kilometres of water and the main lake is a massive 160 miles from western end to the dam in the east. The dam drives the largest hydro-electric plant in Southern Africa.

From the border to Songo, the lower plains had looked much more friendly than the mountains, but at Songo the landscape rose up again. Just two hours after rolling off Harare he crossed into Malawi and almost immediately was talking to Kamuzu International (FWKI), and soon passed the city of Lilongwe on his starboard side. The airport was still above 4000 feet so little descent was needed, and twenty minutes later he was on right base for runway 14 – nicely into wind and more than two miles long. Landing on the "piano keys" it was an early turn-off to the terminal.

Mike Gray had been right – it was a good place to lay over, with efficient fuelling and immigration clearance. Moreover, whilst most hotels with shuttle buses were in Lilongwe, 12 or more miles away, the Orisons Guest House was just two miles from the airport and a mere $30. Once unpacked (which took just seconds as he was so light) and after putting all his equipment on charge, he called ATC back at Harare to ask about the phone call they had received as he was leaving.

Apparently, the call had come in just as they were changing over duty controller, so although the new man on duty hadn't taken the call himself, he did know that it was something about wanting to buy the Robin - "Sorry, that's all I know". Very, very strange thought Martin before he commenced his flight planning for the next day, and later called home.

Saturday 8 April 2023 – an easy day?

Dodoma in Tanzania was only 485NM away by his chosen route, but the following leg to Lokichogio would be 634NM. It was just too much for one day, so Martin had resigned himself to just reaching Dodoma.

A leisurely breakfast was on the cards and his hosts took good care of him starting with a muesli yoghurt, which was followed by a full English (or should that be full Malawi?). Once sated, packed and paid he decided to walk the 2 miles back to the airport. It was still early and cool enough to do so as it at this time of year the temperature was similar to that at home. The exercise would do him good, and besides, he'd be sat in the aircraft for around four hours.

As he walked, he reflected on the route he had planned. Whilst he could have flown a straight line to Dodoma it would have meant more than 111NM over the water of Lake Malawi. If the Cahora Bassa had looked big, this was enormous. The whole lake was 500NM long and even if he crossed it diagonally, at some stage he would be 15NM from the nearest shore, and with the Robin's glide ratio of only 9.3 (his Cessna was 12), he would need an enormous height to make the shore if the engine failed - and even the shoreline wasn't low. Rough calculations had meant he would need to be somewhere near 10,000 feet to be safe, and he didn't have oxygen.

Better to have added a few miles and route up the western side of the lake, which also had the bonus of keeping him away from Mozambique airspace. Although he already had an overflying permit, he wasn't sure if it allowed two entries and he'd already done one.

Once at the airport, he needed to settle up and pass through immigration again. After advice he had applied and paid online for a transit visa at $50. This was valid for seven days and $25 cheaper than a single entry – he didn't need three months! The highest other fee was $40 navigation charge (International) but landing and parking only totalled $13, and he was delighted to have avoided the handling charge of $450. Even the fuel was a pleasant surprise with PUMA's service charge actually less for Avgas, than for Jet A-1.

Strapping himself into the Robin, he reflected that his new British Passport (that had replaced the previous EU variety) was certainly getting some exotic stamps in it. Checks complete, he called Lumbadzi Tower on 118.700 and was ready to go. There was no need to take the taxiway to the runway threshold as taxying straight from apron across the taxiway and onto the runway still gave him 2500m available for take-off, which he duly did.

Once established in the climb off runway 14 a left turn took him onto a heading of 020 to pass overhead the airfield at Ntchisi (FWCS). As always, he would route overhead or very close to any available airfields in case of problems. He would then route to Mzuku (FWKK) passing over the Nkotakhota Wildlife Reserve, and then really begin to climb as SkyDemon had told him of a necessary safety height of 9000 feet as he approached Karonga (FWKA). As he was flying under visual flight rules, 8500 feet would suffice, but as he then crossed the tip of Lake Malawi the highest peaks were in front of him, and he'd need 9700 feet.

Flying virtually due north now, the Robin's engine purred along beautifully as they passed over the wildlife – but at this height nothing could be seen. By contrast the massive Lake Malawi filled his view to the right. It wasn't a great deal more than an hour before he overflew Mzuzu, the third largest city in Malawi and one he had never heard of before last week. Nestling in the midst of the city (at 4,115 feet ASL) was the 1300m asphalt airfield – very adequate had he had need of it.

Shortly after Mzuzu on his right was the North Vipya Firing Range (FWD1) which NOTAMs had not shown as active today. With a base at 5000 feet, it reaches FL230, so heaven knows what they fire there? And then it was overhead the restricted area at Nyiku National Park, but he was so high for the coming mountains it was way below him. Two hours after take-off he was passing overhead Karonga (or Lapangan Terbang Karonga to give its full name). It was almost on the shore of Lake Malawi and at only 1765 feet, but he was still edging upwards to 9700 feet for that last mountain to cross.

It was only 30NM more to the tip of the lake at Matema, and the crossing into Dar Es Salaam airspace. Then the highest peaks were soon all around as he passed through the Rungwe volcanic range. Rungwe itself (2960m) was northwest and the nearest peak to his right was Ihobwela (2312m) but the whole area was high and uninviting. Not the place to have an engine problem – only choice would be to turn around and glide back to the lake, but the high range was wide and that wouldn't always be a possibility.

FREDA checks and changing fuel tanks had kept him busy from time to time, but he hadn't been bored as he had never seen scenery like it – or even been that high except in commercial aircraft. Not quite true as he had once climbed to 10,000 feet when his Cessna had the old Continental O-300D engine, and it had taken an eternity to reach that height. On that occasion he was so high above the ground it felt as if he wasn't moving, but now he was close to the peaks and with the help of a tailwind had a much better impression of progress.

But he still had two hours to run to Domeda and was beginning to wonder if he should have fitted the "Urination Management" equipment before commencing the flight. He knew he'd need it for the next few flights but had put off for as long as possible – apart from which, walking from Guest House to airport wouldn't have been comfortable, and although he could have used the conveniences at the airport, he preferred to test himself today.

Shortly after leaving the tip of Lake Malawi at Matema, he finally crossed the highest mountains on his path, and soon was between two high ridges with nothing between them higher than 5000 feet. Furthermore, another enormous lake appeared below him, to be replaced by the arid plateau that is central Tanzania. Scorched ground still produced grass and occasional wooded areas and the tracks of dry riverbeds could be seen by the vegetation that followed their curves.

It still made sense to stay high as the tailwind was helping, and besides, when he reached Dodoma Airport it would be at 3,637 feet, and whilst it had lowered, the terrain still did not look inviting. As he had left the lake, he'd reported his border crossing to Dar Information on 123.300 and given his estimate for Dodoma. Told to report when 50 miles to run to HTDO, he had nothing to but to manage the fuel tanks and think about his bladder. Oh, to be in England where you could let down into a friendly airstrip for a comfort break!

He was only halfway from the lake to Dodoma and was in pain. He never drank coffee when about to fly as he knew it was a diuretic, and had only allowed himself one tea today, but whether it was the pitch of the Robin's engine, the altitude, or whatever, he knew he wouldn't make Dodoma. The Great Ruaha River was paralleling his track and mercifully SkyDemon announced that he was approaching an airstrip. He hadn't been aware when planning, but now opened his Android Pad and zoomed in the screen to find Ruaha (HTMR) was very close to his track to the left. The only information offered was that it was a gravel strip running 11/29 and 1212m long. No radio, no admin information – but it would have to do.

He couldn't just disappear from radar so called Dar Information to explain he needed to make a precautionary landing and would call them once on the ground and inform them of his intentions if he could "clear the problem". Once Dar had established that he wasn't declaring an emergency, they agreed to inform the expectant Dodoma Airport and update them once they heard from him on the ground. With that, he concentrated on a rapid descent to 4000 feet until the strip came into view. The strip was at 2635 feet, and he joined left base for runway 29 with his eyes peeled for any traffic, but there was none to be seen and nothing showing on SkyEcho/SkyDemon ADS-B.

As he was touching down, some 600m to the right of the threshold there were buildings and a hangar with a Cessna Caravan outside. He'd need to visit to explain his arrival, but before then he reached the western end of the strip, shut down the engine and poured himself out of the aircraft. Within yards was an acacia tree, and perfect for him to relieve himself against. Never again, he vowed.

Back in the aircraft he started up and back tracked the runway to the hangar, where he was greeted by a ranger in a pick-up truck "Welcome to Msembe!". After offering an apology for his unexpected arrival, Martin discovered that he was at the headquarters of Ruaha National Park and fortunately there were no airspace restrictions due wildlife.

Reginald, the ranger, had introduced himself and explained that Msembe was the local name for the strip, whilst the ICAO name was Ruaha and that was used by the two airlines that operated charters into the game park. Both Auric Air and Coastal Aviation had 16 Cessna Caravan 208B apiece, but the Caravan parked by the hangar was 5H-LOL - a Grand Caravan operated by Safari Air Link.

After Martin had explained the need to call back to Dar Information on a landline (his sim was not connecting his mobile to local coverage), he was taken to the office and allowed to call them. "I'm pretty sure the blockage is cleared now, and I'll just check everything again, and then set off for Dodoma – I'll call you as soon as airborne". It wasn't completely a lie, and he knew he needed to relax a little more before committing aviation again.

It would only be a little less than an hour to Dodoma (and he would only need to climb to 5300 feet) so was happy to accept the offered cup of tea from Reginald. "You could always stay over in one of the units and go for a game drive in the morning" was the second offer, but Martin wasn't sure what trouble he would be in already for landing at a non-customs airport and besides, Jean would be expecting a call on his arrival at Dodoma.

With that he thanked Reginald and walked back down to the hangar and readied the Robin. Whilst SkyDemon had said the strip was gravel, it was in fact hard-packed red earth, and the looser dust now covered the aircraft, and the windscreen needed cleaning gently. Hopefully it would blow off the wings once in the air. The Caravan showed no evidence of same, but then it was a high-wing aircraft and much taller generally.

With his "Check A" completed he taxied back to the threshold of runway 29 and pointed the nose at the brush to the side of the runway whilst doing power checks so as not to pull more dust towards him. A wave to the watching Reginald, and he was off and as he climbed skywards, reflected on his "easy day" so far…….

Dodoma Arrival

Once on a track of 030 magnetic both SkyDemon and the Garmin told him he had just 54 minutes to run, and he called Dar Information to pass the news. They would inform Dodoma of his impending arrival and asked him to call again with 50 miles to run, which he duly did. Just on the half hour he was transferred to Dodoma Tower on 133.000, who informed him of runway 27 being in use and there being no wind to speak of.

Dodoma is the capital of Tanzania and the 2503m runway is right in the middle of the city. Despite being surrounded by 325,000 residents there were no noise abatement procedures except that there is no night-flying except in emergency. But it's a large city with little chance of finding an emergency landing area, so Martin stayed high until on short final, then dropped full flaps and even used a little sideslip. Probably not recommended but it never lost rudder authority in his Cessna and didn't now.

He was directed to the terminal, which was off to the right, two-thirds along the runway and was a low corrugated iron roofed building. There were two other aircraft there, the first an Air Tanzania Bombardier Dash 8 and the second had a very strange airline name. It was an ATR 72 – with HOP!-REGIONAL emblazoned on the fuselage. He supposed that it probably "does what it says on the tin"……….

By the time he had shut down, recorded times, and reached the step on the wing, a small reception committee was around the aircraft. Friendly enough, but very interested in why he had had to put down at Msembe and had he left anything there? Once he had come clean, they were amused but still wanted to check the contents of his luggage (what little there was) and of course quizzed him about the condom catheter and piping they found, and again smiled at the explanation. "You will know better next time!" "Certainly will – tomorrow's leg is six hours".

Paperwork completed he settled the landing and parking fees which were extremely reasonable – at under 2000Kg landing was a mere $9 and the first two hours were free with another 12 hours for $5. Mike Gray had chosen well. The representative of Aviary who Mike had arranged for fuel and handling arrived and explained he would have to reposition to the GA area, slightly east of the main terminal and would meet him there. After taxying there he was the only non-metal aircraft to be seen. 3 Cessnas – 172, 182 and 206, a Beech Baron, and a beefy Cessna Chancellor twin were alongside him and the other side of the taxiway was an abandoned Antonov AN28 of the Tanzanian Air Force.

Aviary arrived with the Avgas bowser and Martin ensured every tank was filled to the brim – he'd need it! Although he'd been expecting it, the fueller (Robert) was keen to hear about what a small South African-registered aircraft was doing there, particularly with an English pilot. He was somewhat impressed by the explanation of what would end up being a rather epic journey for one inexperienced in Africa. His English was perfect, and he obviously wanted to chat and tell of the history of Aviary and the airport. Apparently when a colony (Tanganyika), during World War 2, the British had established the airport with a 500m grass runway. It had grown from there and after independence, Air Tanzania came into existence as did Precision Air (with 40% Kenyan ownership).

The only really bad history was a Precision Air ATR42 (5H-PWF) that had crashed trying to land at Bukoba. In bad weather it ended up in Lake Victoria and all 19 aboard drowned including the two pilots. Otherwise, the airport had continued to expand, and the government had decided to buy 2 Boeing 737s direct from Boeing – but it remains to be seen if Dodoma is long enough for them to operate safely.

After ensuring Martin's education had been improved, Robert was good enough to give him a lift to "Baobob Home Stay" a nearby guest house and a bargain at $32. Although it was only walking distance from the airport it would have been hard for him to find. Once ensconced in his room, Martin was grateful for the Wi-Fi as his SIM still wouldn't connect, and at least he could email Jean and tell of the day's "adventure". Then it was the usual routine - eat, plan, sleep – it would be an early start.

Sunday 9 April 2023

Were he to have planned a direct line to Lokichogio (HKLK) he could have reached there in 629NM, but to avoid entering Uganda airspace a tiny dogleg was required, and it only added some 6NM. Soon after entering Kenyan airspace, he would overfly Oseur airfield and later Eldoret International and then the mission airfield at Alale. But first he needed to prep.

Having gone through the paperwork and formalities, his last item before boarding his aircraft was to visit the gents and fit the catheter and drainage system – yesterday's fiasco was not to be repeated! This wasn't to be the longest day and with no wind forecast he could probably reach today's destination in just over five hours (and he'd budgeted for six). So, with virtually no surface wind, he lined up on 09 directly from the GA area and had about two-thirds of the 2500m runway available.

After lifting off, a left turn took him onto a heading of 356 magnetic, and he began to climb. He was tracking a high volcanic ridge and whilst the first half-hour was over ground at about 8000 feet, he knew what was coming so climbed to 9300 and still felt very close to the peaks that appeared to the sides of his track, and which at Ngorongora were 10,551 feet to the left and 11,969 feet to the right. But these paled into insignificance once he glimpsed Kilimanjaro in the distance. Despite being 100 miles to his right, the air was clear enough that he could see it rising to 19,341 feet – the highest mountain/volcano in Africa. Amazing that so many people actually trek to the top, he thought – especially those celebrities who do so for charity and presumably have little training?

He was still thinking about it as he had to call Nairobi Centre on 118.500 whilst crossing into Kenya, and within minutes was overhead the airfield at Oseur. He knew it was there as SkyDemon told him so (and even got an audible warning of "airfield below") but he was damned if he could see it.

Supposedly, it was 3600 feet below him and would be 950m of grass should he need it, but he couldn't see anything green in the surrounding area that could be called grass! Still, if the donkey stopped, he would aim for it and hopefully it would become more obvious…….

As he'd passed the Kenyan border, he'd changed tanks for the second time and was now more than two hours into the flight. Out to his left by some seventy miles was Lake Victoria – the second largest freshwater lake in the world (second to Lake Superior in North America). It was 5600 feet below him and stretched away to the west and covered some 23 square miles. Before he passed over Eldoret International he would only be 25 miles away from the eastern edge. "Mere mortals don't see sights like this" he told himself – it was an expression he jokingly used with his passengers back in UK, but now he really felt it – and it was only day three!

Soon he was talking to Eldoret Approach on 119.400 as he entered their TMA and could make out Kusumi International Airport just adjacent to the eastern "spur" of Lake Victoria that he was close to. Shortly after, and 24 miles before he would reach Eldoret, he was crossing the equator – another aviation first for his logbook.

He had checked how easy it would be to pass over Eldoret and learned there were few passenger flights from there. The "International" title of Eldoret really referred to cargo flights that entered the country there, whereas the airline flights were really shuttles to Nairobi, Kusumi or Lodwar. Sure enough, clearance overhead was forthcoming, and he passed above the 3475m runway 08/26.

The highest peaks were now below 8000 feet, but he kept altitude as would need it at Alale, the adjacent peaks both within a few feet of 9000, albeit to the right of track. Then he was tracking alongside the Greek River which formed the border with Uganda, another country that he didn't want to visit. Whether it was the nearness of the water, or the near four hours he'd been flying, it was time to use the "urination management" equipment, and he simply "let go". Just as in his home trial, it was strange to feel the warmth run down his leg, but at least it was confined to the pipe and everything remained dry, and comfort was resumed.

At Alele he could see the grass strip. Despite it being just under 800m long, it stood out against the scrub that it divided and was alongside the school for girls that was run by the Catholic Mission to Amakuriat. Less than an hour to run and he was looking forward to a beer.

Lokichogio was surrounded by a danger area, and he needed to call Loki Tower on 118.900 for entry and was soon in the descent, the airport being at 2116 feet. Left base onto runway 27 and despite his tiredness he made a reasonable landing. Again, there had been little wind to challenge him. As he rolled to a stop, by the side of the runway was an aircraft graveyard with six recognisable hulks there - various Antonov machines, a Douglas DC-6, and a pile of scrap that could have once been a DC-3.

When he had researched Lokichogio he'd found an interesting history. Originally built for the Kenyan Air Force, it had developed as a humanitarian centre and had been greatly used by the Sudanese Peoples Liberation Army. United Nations operated from there on peace-keeping missions. More recently it had been redeveloped with runway extension and terminal buildings and with its military associations it was a very secure environment. As part of the process many abandoned aircraft were auctioned off in 2021. The Kenya Airports Authority had offered 73 airframes located across four airports for sale at knockdown prices just to clear the land. There had been eleven at Loki, so the remainers obviously got no offers – despite the

DC-6 being only £350! Unsurprising really, as elsewhere there were Boeing 737s at £2,700 and a DC-9 at £740.

Martin surmised that the pile of wreckage was probably the turboprop DC-3 he had read about. South African registered, ZS-KCV had crashed on take-off, rolling over and onto a Cessna Caravan. On investigation it was found that the tail rudder clamp was still in place.

Backtracking runway 27, when he reached the end, it was a starboard turn into the international parking area. Had he continued straight ahead he would have reached the domestic area where he could see a C-130 Hercules. On parking he was alongside 2 PC-12s – his favourite aircraft that he would never afford. Whilst he was in view of the terminal, once everything was shut down, he stayed behind the aircraft and released the stopcock of the bag strapped to his ankle and the waste was gone, and no-one was any wiser. "Thank you, SOSA" he thought – the Canadian gliding club had given great advice about equipment.

Once through security and immigration (his visa was an eTA - electronic Travel Authorisation - paid online the previous week and $69) it was a few short steps to the airport hotel. Basic accommodation but it saved need for transport and an early start would be easy. Checked in he realised it was even more basic than expected and had no wi-fi, so it was necessary to return to the terminal business centre to research weather, file tomorrow's flightplan, and most importantly email Jean with his progress. The beauty of email was that he could go into detail without worrying about phone roaming charges building up, so he could mention most of the day's adventure.

Having said that Martin realised he was starving and still hadn't had the beer he'd promised himself, so he would go to the airport restaurant and remedy the situation but return later to see if Jean had answered. Refuelling the Robin would be done in the morning. He would want it filled to the gills, and then leave immediately so the Avgas would not have time to expand in the morning heat and vent through the overflow. Flamex Petroleum would be the supplier, and they would bring the bowser to him at 09.00 local time.

His meal was pleasant enough despite airport pricing, and his second beer really hit the spot.

Monday 10 April 2023

This was the big one. A full 700NM and no SkyDemon chart for Sudan to help. The Garmin GPS could get him there provided there were no satellite problems and as back up there was a high altitude VOR at Kenana – but that was 545NM to the north of Loki. Whilst no mapping for Sudan could be seen on SkyDemon it had made sense to plot waypoints for the turning points and destination, and despite no mapping, SkyDemon still produced a pilot log which importantly showed safety altitudes, as well as factoring current winds to give leg times.

Martin entered these into his manually created PLOG adjusting them by 500 feet as he would be VFR. Then came the rub, the projected time to reach Khartoum was 393 minutes or 6 hours 33 minutes. With full fuel of 240 litres at 33 litres per hour, he would have just 7 hours 16 minutes even if every drop was usable. With nowhere else to go within half an hour, what if something stopped him landing at Khartoum?

He had to be certain of the weather and searched everything he could find, and it all looked remarkably similar – a gentle northerly flow would be against him as intimated by SkyDemon, but at least the destination was clear with only 5% chance of precipitation. This was as expected for the advancing monsoon season (it would be soon as it was April), but when he checked the Windy App he discovered that at a decent height the wind could become from the south-west at around 15 knots. Checking SkyDemon again, their PLOG had used his standard operational height in UK – 2000 feet.

After adjusting the figures, by flying at 8000 feet the difference would be amazing, and the small tailwind would bring him to just over five hours. Even if it wasn't as strong or was more easterly it would still be a go. Decision made, it was through security to the aircraft and a final check of everything. Although the dipstick showed it had hardly used any oil, he thought it wise to top up the Aeroshell 15w-50 with a quart which he obtained from the Flamex bowser when it arrived – and bought a couple more in case needed and not available en route.

Bills settled by card, he strapped in and radioed Loki Tower to request start. There was nothing behind him, so he did power and control checks where he was and then taxied just a few yards to the threshold of runway 27. No fuel wasted, cleared for take-off immediately and he was accelerating down the runway. As he lifted off the DC-6 was off to his right and he thought that had it been in the UK for £350, the front half of it would have made a great motorcaravan.

No time for dreaming – he needed to get high quickly so began cruise-climbing to the north squeezing between the mountain range to his starboard and the Uganda border to port. In just 24NM he reached the Kenya/Sudan border and turned onto 333 magnetic. He would keep this heading for 208NM before turning north. This would dogleg him around the westernmost part of Ethiopia for which he had no overflying permit and was also quite mountainous.

The difference in scenery was startling. Having traversed high volcanic regions, once he had passed over Boma National Park he was flying over low-lying marshlands and there was just nothing to be seen from 8000 feet. Nicely trimmed-out the Robin purred along, and he was gratified to see a groundspeed of 135 knots indicated by both GPS and SkyDemon. All he had to do was keep remembering to change tanks and do his FREDA checks.

He'd just changed tanks for the second time, having used both wing tanks, and had turned to main tank - only it suddenly went very quiet. The engine coughed just once, and he was gliding. Stupid, stupid……he had turned the fuel cock the wrong way. It was the opposite of his Cessna – the "off" position on the

Robin was at the top, whereas on his Cessna it was at the bottom (with the top position being "both"). A swift 180 degree turn of the fuel cock and fuel pump on (he wouldn't need the latter in the Cessna – indeed it didn't have one) and the O-360 kicked back into life. Martin had lost just two hundred feet, but an enormous amount of pride in his flying skills.

"Doh! Doh! Doh!" he said, realising he had become Homer Simpson. Was he just tired? Or was it the boredom of nothing to see and no-one to talk to, to keep him sharp? He reflected that he just wasn't used to such long flights, and in UK airspace there's always something to keep the pilot alert. "Never again" – it was the second use of the phrase this week.

Once on a northerly heading it was interesting to see how soon the KNA VOR would register on his OBS. He dialled up 115.400, set the OBS to north, and then waited for the flag to drop. It was going to be quite a wait as from the turn he had 314NM to run to the beacon, and he didn't really expect to get the possible 200NM range – although there were no obstructions to the line-of-sight transmission.

By the time it came within range, the marshy lowlands had changed to dry, flat savannah, and before he reached the beacon, he had been roughly following the White Nile as it made its way north from Lake Victoria to pass through Khartoum - where it would meet the Blue Nile on its way to Alexandria. Now the land was irrigated and had more interest.

Around the beacon, his sectional chart showed a group of three airfields. There was Kenana itself very near the beacon and operated by the Kenana Sugar Corporation. Kenana Air Base was a little further out and used by the Sudan Air Force with their Antonovs, and Kenana East further still and that could not be seen. But any would have done in an emergency.

It would be a little over an hour from here to the VOR (KTM) two miles south of Khartoum, and Martin concentrated on staying awake and doing all the right things. These included feasting on a granola bar as he hoped it would increase his alertness – didn't need any more mistakes! It was quite a pleasant temperature in the cabin at 23 degrees, which meant he was expecting nearly 40 degrees on the ground.

Having talked to approach on 124.700 he was passed to the tower on 119.200 before he overflew the VOR. By then the 3043m runway was directly in front of him and he was lined up for a runway 36 approach. Now he had descended he had a gentle northerly headwind of just 8 knots and made a greaser of a landing. "About time you got something right" he told himself.

Welcome to Sudan

Mike Gray had given Martin several warnings about Khartoum. Firstly, that paperwork had to be perfectly correct, and that although he already had a visa from the Sudanese Embassy in London, he might be asked to pay for an exit visa as he left. More importantly, he had warned that the country was becoming even more politically unstable, and Martin needed to be ready to take an alternative route should he read or hear anything worrying in the days before his arrival.

It was one thing to say that, but without alternative overflight permits and handling arrangements in place, where would he go? But the papers and television had not mentioned anything, so here he was. Having landed on 36, it was a left turn into the terminal areas, which surprised him by its size and the amount of airline traffic which was coming and going to such a relatively poor country. Before he had disembarked and was hit by the heat reflected off the concrete, a 4x4 Mercedes emblazoned with "Airspace Aviation Services" had drawn up alongside. This was the agent that Mike had insisted he needed – for safety as much efficiency. Zahid Ishmael introduced himself and explained he would take care of everything.

This included driving him (happily in air-conditioning) to the General Aviation reception area where documentation and passport were thoroughly examined, and an extraordinary amount of dollars were requested for the landing fee. Martin had never heard of negotiating a landing fee, but that's just what Zahid proceeded to do and after pointing out the low weight of the aircraft and how it was private not commercial, managed to bargain down to a mere $250. It hadn't cost much more than that when he had once landed at Stansted!

He already knew that Zahid's handling fee would be another $200 and that he had pre-paid Mike for the landing *permit* (equivalent of another $100) – it was starting to look like the most expensive stopover in the world, and that was before he found an hotel. Again, Zahid came up trumps. He wouldn't allow Martin to go anywhere as the nearest was 2 miles from the airport and he deemed it too dangerous an area, even if he was driving. Better that he accepted the spare room offered and meet Zahid's family, which he duly did.

They were lovely people, the house was spick and span, and the accommodation adequate. Dinner was a welcoming affair, and he was given generous helpings of lamb kamounia – which he had never heard of but was delicious. The children wanted to speak English which they did well as they were originally from South Sudan where it is an official language. Now they lived in Khartoum, Arabic was the norm, so practice was appreciated. The whole evening was a delight, the only downside for Martin being a complete lack of alcohol, but no doubt he could catch up over the next few days.

Tuesday 11 April 2023

Once back at the airport and away from the children, Zahid shared his worries about the near future, whilst Mathew Petroleum Company refuelled the Robin under his watchful eye.

Whilst Martin knew of Sudan, he knew little of its history but had heard of long conflicts since its independence – indeed his last visited airfield, Lokichogio, had been a base for the attempted peacekeepers. Apparently, Khartoum Airport was established by the RAF in 1940 as a base called Gordon's Tree and where Vickers Wellesleys and Curtis Tomahawks were based. At one stage there were 50 Harvards and 20 Hurricanes there too. Sudan gained independence in 1956 and it then became both a civil airport and military base.

Various military factions grew throughout the country, and it adopted Islamic law. Thirty years of military dictatorship led by Omar Al-Bashir came to an end in 2020 but not before widespread persecution of minorities and even genocide in Darfur. Supposedly it then began a transition to democratic rule, but the power was still held by members of the militia, and recently they had started arguing amongst themselves. Zahid had fears of what would happen in the next few months, or even weeks, but like his fellow countrymen there was little opportunity for escape or even movement to safer areas. Anything that was likely to happen would start in Khartoum where the military factions were ensconced, but "inshallah" his fears might be unfounded.

For a poor nation, they had certainly learnt how to help richer nations distribute their wealth. The fees so far had been bad enough, but the Avgas price was eye-watering. But there wasn't an alternative source, and they knew it. Zahid had proved himself to be a real gentleman – welcoming, hospitable and invaluable at keeping costs down, and Martin safe. So much so that once plans were filed and he'd been able to email Jean (there had been no internet at Zahid's) he'd paid the exit visa, and once he had been delivered back to the apron, Martin gave him a large tip (not quite as much he had saved on the landing fee, but significant, and in USD) and wished him well for the future.

I hope he is wrong about there being forthcoming trouble, he thought. Then he fired up the Robin's Lycoming engine. The Canadian recommended equipment had been fitted in the comfort of the air-conditioned terminal, and he knew he'd need it again today. The flight to Hurghada (HEGN) was virtually the same as yesterday's – 700NM non-stop – or at least that was the plan.

The forecast winds at height seemed to vary somewhat. Supposedly he would start with a headwind approaching nine knots, but as he crossed into Egypt after 3 hours 10 minutes, there would be a an almost westerly wind, effectively neutral to his airspeed, and he would reach Hurghada after another 2 hours 30 minutes. It might have been worse, and if he went higher than necessary his True Air Speed could improve. Just as importantly, he would be cooler – he was already starting to bake in the cockpit - despite there being a large fan in front of him. Were he in his Cessna, he would have had a sunshade due the high wing (and an umbrella in the opposite kind of weather) but the low-wing Robin provided neither.

After climbing off the northerly runway, he gained height following the Nile for some thirty miles before it swung to the northeast. He would meet it again once he was in Egypt and would parallel Lake Nasser before it reached Aswan. Cruise-climbing, he was heading for FL90 to comply with the semi-circular rule (his true track was 005) and as he climbed there seemed to be no change in the headwind component. Excellent. He could lean and conserve more fuel at height and the cabin was getting cooler.

It needed to, as when he had passed the line of latitude at 19 degrees north of the equator, he was overhead the desert. Completely barren and under a clear sky, it must have baking on the ground. Funny how things work out – had it been two months later he would have risked violent dust storms caused by the "haboob" winds. All he needed to do now was fly straight, change tanks (correctly), and stay alert. In some ways it was good that he didn't have the luxury of an autopilot or wing-leveller, otherwise he could easily have dozed off with no-one to talk to.

As before, there was no mapping on SkyDemon for either Sudan or Egypt, but he had plotted the waypoints and had the Garmin set up. Whilst tracking away from Khartoum he used the VOR there for as long as it was in range and knew that at some stage, he would pick up ASN (the Aswan VOR on 112.300). He wouldn't overfly Aswan as he wanted to keep as straight a line as possible, but it would assure him of position in case of any GPS fall-out. Similarly, the Hurghada VOR on 116.500 (HGD) would lead him to the airport.

After what seemed an endless three hours, he was ready to call Cairo FIR and shortly after entry the landscape began to change. Whilst still not particularly high, there was higher ground off to his right in between his track and the Red Sea, and soon he was alongside Lake Nasser which occupied what used to be the Nubian Valley. Whilst the dam was being created it was necessary to move the population of some 100,000 people to new locations, such as New Nubia, but Martin was unaware of its history, and simply paralleled the lake and then the Nile as it made its way to Luxor. He still wasn't picking up the VOR at Hurghada, but both SkyDemon and GPS were keeping him on track, and as he swung past Aswan with that VOR dialled up, the flag switched over from TO to FROM.

The Nile was less than 40 miles to his port side but once he passed the dam it was hard to see, and he could see nothing of the temples prior to Luxor that others would pay a fortune to visit. Couldn't be helped – even a small sightseeing diversion would use extra fuel and add time. The leg needed to be finished and now he could pick up the Hurghada VOR to lead him to the airport.

Approach frequency was 123.400 and as soon as he called, he was told to expect a hold due to incoming jet traffic. The surface wind had turned more southerly, and they were using Runway 16R, the wider of the two new runways. There was a flow of arrivals including EasyJet and Whizz Air and he was instructed to cross the airfield west to east at 2000 feet (airfield elevation was 52 feet), and then to hold over Zuzar Abu Minqar – the small island just off the coast. After what seemed an interminable number of orbits, and with his eyes constantly checking the fuel state, they found him a gap, and passed him to the tower on 119.600.

Tower instructed a left base join to 16L so that if he was too slow, 16R could be used by commercial traffic. The runways were actually a kilometre apart, so at least the nearer runway would save him some taxying time, and whilst 16L was 45 metres wide compared to 16R's 60 metres, it was ample, and the Robin quickly touched down and turned off and then onto the parallel taxiway (which used to be the old runway before development).

Ground on 121.900 directed him to Terminal 1, the older terminal and at the top of the airfield so again his taxi time was saved. Once the Lycoming was shut down, a people carrier arrived with a plethora of officials to examine the paperwork. Everything was in order and filed in sequence so that if a full ramp check was instigated (53 items might be checked!) then it would be obvious after the first few sheets that he had done his homework, and hopefully they would curtail the investigation. And so it was.

They were good enough to give a lift to the terminal and he really appreciated the air-conditioning. Once through immigration (his visa had been bought via the visa2egypt portal before leaving UK) he searched and eventually found the Nile Valley Aviation desk. Mike Gray had suggested them as the only FBO who regularly had Avgas available, and when he had checked a week ago, they did. Ahmed, the receptionist, was extremely apologetic. They had run out just the previous day and having clients expected over the next few days (Martin included) had organised some 100LL to be sent down from Cairo. This would have to be in barrels and transported down by truck as their bowser was under repair – the journey by road would be five hours and it would leave tomorrow and arrive before the end of Wednesday.

"We could get some Mogas for you if that would help you reach your next stopover" he offered. Martin thought about it, but only for a few moments. Whilst there were many STCs that allowed Mogas to be used in Lycoming engines, he was certain no-one would have issued one for a Robin. Todd Petersen in USA was the main source of Mogas STCs and had probably never even seen a Robin. With no paperwork he would invalidate his temporary insurance, and who knows what effect the temperature would have – he'd heard of vapour locks caused by Mogas (and yet he'd once flown a 172 in Dubai that ran on Mogas – there is no Avgas in the Emirates).

"Are you certain it will arrive tomorrow?" Ahmed was but couldn't guarantee at what time. Tomorrow was to be another long flight, and a lot over water, so another good reason not to risk Mogas. There was nothing for it, but to stay over an extra day. With that he went to find the terminal hospitality desk where they could find him a local hotel for two nights. Bugger!

Once the desk attendant understood that he wasn't on holiday and just wanted somewhere to stopover and with peace and quiet to plan, Martin was soon offered Sunshine Holidays

Resort. It was an adults-only hotel, so peace should be assured as long as his room wasn't above a disco or barbeque or something. He felt that an extra good night's rest and a relaxing day would do him good, and it wasn't that expensive.

The airport taxi only took fifteen minutes to reach Sheraton Road where the hotel overlooked a private lagoon. Having asked that his room would not be above anything noisy, he soon found himself with a lovely sea view overlooking the very island he had been orbiting over, for so long earlier that day. There were lots of facilities he could take advantage of, including multiple charging points for all his equipment, decent wi-fi, and importantly an overnight laundry service where he immediately committed his shirts and underwear.

Once that was set in motion, he thought about planning the next leg and was gratified that the next flight would end in Europe, so he was free of the need for overflight permissions once there. There wasn't any point in filing a flight plan until he was certain of Avgas and had threatened Ahmed that he would call him regularly until he was told it had arrived.

He wouldn't be flying tomorrow and could afford to have more than the odd beer that evening, but before then he needed to explain the situation to Jean, and the wi-fi came into its own, and they had a long conversation that by email that would have cost a fortune by phone. Once done, he chose to make his way to the Deuce Sports Bar where he could overlook the ocean – the hotel had six bars and six restaurants, but sitting alone and looking out over the water would suit him. Despite being an Islamic country, and it currently being Ramadan, the hotel was still serving alcohol, for which he was grateful.

Wednesday 12 April 2023 – a day off?

Even though he knew he probably had all day, once breakfast was out of the way, it was time to plan. When he'd originally calculated times and distances he'd thought of a straight line to Crete, but studying the maps and considering fuel burns so far, he could err on the side of caution and planned so that he would be over water for as short a time as possible. There was no way he could have brought a life-raft with him, and even if he had bought one, the weight penalty would have been great. Now his planned route would lengthen the flight a little and would be the longest leg, but it would still be possible coming in at 721NM.

Importantly, he would fly northwest until he reached the coast at Sidi Baranni which was just east of the Libyan border which he didn't want to cross. From there it would be almost due north for 205NM over water, to coast in at Crete and overfly the military base at Kasteli, then northwest again to Iraklion. By doglegging he would avoid the Restricted Area south of Iraklion that was shown on SkyDemon. It was so nice to have up-to-date information again now the area was covered by his favourite software!

On reflection, he realised that he had flown over some very large stretches of water before, a good example being a flight to Herning in Denmark for a Precision Flying competition. Then it had been twice the distance now envisaged, but with the benefit of passing near Groningen halfway along.

With the turning points entered he realised he needed to consider wind strength. The prevailing wind in Egypt is from the northwest – perfectly against the first 493NM and still with (but a lesser) headwind element for the northern track. Anything over 15 knots would reduce his planned reserve fuel and could even make him breach the legal limit of a half-hour reserve. With more than 24 hours to go, he couldn't make the go/no-go decision until he saw the forecasts on the day. Again, it was a good job he wasn't under the cosh of a dated overflight permit, as his extra overnight stop might turn into more.

With initial planning in place, he thought he might as well enjoy the facilities and took a position on the sundeck where he could watch the beach and look out to sea. Very soon he was musing about how many countries he had visited when he was working, and Egypt wasn't one of them. His viewpoint looked out across the Strait of Jubal, which lead to the Gulf of Suez and of course, the canal. It was less than fifty miles across the water to Sharm El Sheikh and beyond that was the Gulf of Aqaba where he had been before. Shortly after he and Jean married, they had visited Jordan (with his parents) to see his sister Barbara.

Barbara had been working there for Telecom, but her real purpose there had been being part of a Christian Mission team, based near Amman. It was a somewhat risky business and within a couple of years, the Islamic Brotherhood got to hear of the organisation, and she was forced to up sticks and move to Cyprus for safety. There she continued her work, keeping contact with the converts she had made.

Before that happened, during the family's visit, they had driven the length of the Kings Highway from Amman to Aqaba, some 200 miles which doesn't sound far, but included negotiating various Wadis enroute. They stopped first at the Dead Sea, where bathing was an unusual experience. Firstly because of the way the girls had to be shielded by the boys with towels as they got into the water – to protect them from the crowds of local men who came to ogle. Once in the water the salt concentration was so high, sinking was impossible and your whole body popped up to the surface, and you could lie horizontally with no need to move. On leaving the water, the boys had to get out first so that the shielding could be repeated. It was a far cry from the beach here at Hurghada, where nobody blinked an eye at a bikini.

Further down the Kings Highway they had stopped at Petra, riding into the carved city on horseback. Many years later Harrison Ford would do the same in his role of Indiana Jones!

After leaving Petra, Martin's father Bernard had become more and more unwell with a stomach bug (probably from a "dirty" salad) and by Aqaba looked as if he would die. Barbara had high up friends in Jordan, in that she and Prince Hassan had conversed regularly by amateur radio, which she had needed because of the remoteness of her accommodation. She once had badly cut her hand opening a can and could not stop the blood flow. Sending an SOS to anyone that could hear her, she was answered by Prince Hassan who was a ham enthusiast, and he immediately organised help and a medic. Since then, they had spoken regularly, and now she used her contact to get Bernard into a military hospital.

Completely dehydrated, he was put onto a drip and antibiotics. Being a military hospital there was no nighttime nursing staff, so Barbara stayed in a chair beside him and within 2 days he had made a full recovery, and the family spent time together in Aqaba. Less than 200 miles from where Martin was now, it seemed both a world and a lifetime away.

Sharing a border with Jordan is Israel, and many years later Martin had visited Tel-Aviv briefly for work. Fortunately, his new passport was "clean" with no Israeli stamps, or he would have had trouble gaining entry to some countries.

After a hard day watching couples enjoy themselves when he returned to his room and wi-fi he had a series of messages. The most important was from Ahmed, confirming that the Avgas had arrived, and he would be able to pump from the barrels in the morning – and the earlier the better was a good plan. The next mail was a real surprise – it was from Ron Stirk, his South African engineer. Ron was enquiring where he was. Had he left Sudan yet? "Just need to know you are alright!". That sounded very considerate and deserved an answer, which he gave, explaining that he'd cleared Khartoum nearly two days ago, telling Ron where he was now, and that he'd be leaving for Iraklion next day.

"Thank God for that – have you seen the news?". No, he hadn't but would look at television to see what Ron meant. With Egypt sharing a border with Sudan, it was a big part of the local news – it was rumoured that there was a very likely conflict between the Rapid Support Forces (one branch of Sudan Armed Forces) and the main SAF. Opposing Generals were posturing about who should be in charge of what, and world opinion was suggesting trouble was close. Perhaps Zahid's fears were about to come true. Martin thanked Ron for his concern but assured him he was safe. "I'd hate an aircraft we worked on to be a casualty – and the owner of course" Ron wrote, ending the email with a Smiley. "I'll keep you posted." said Martin.

Thursday 13 April 2023

Having risen early and taken breakfast quickly, Martin was by his aeroplane before the day started to heat up. He'd checked out of the hotel and his luggage was already in the aircraft in the hope that he'd be leaving. Ahmed arrived with a truck containing 4 barrels of Avgas and a suitable pump and shook his hand warmly. Each barrel contained 195 litres so just one might be enough (dependant how much had remained from the previous flight) but he needed to be certain every tank was totally full. At least, fuelling a low-wing Robin was easier than having to pump up fuel into the wing of a Cessna.

Once assured he had the full 240 litres on board, Martin agreed to come back to the Nile Aviation desk to settle up but would first visit Flight Briefing to see the latest weather before he could file a flight plan. He'd checked SkyDemon in the hope that winds would be displayed but the only figures were for his airfield destination and a message was displayed "wind forecasts are not available for your journey, so zero wind has been assumed". Too, too risky – he needed a proper forecast!

The good news at the FBO was that the prevailing northwest wind was likely to be rather less than the limiting 15 knots he had calculated – indeed it wasn't far off the SkyDemon option at less than 10 knots – which slightly disagreed with the local weather at Iraklion - which was showing 12 knots, but after all, the airport is on the coast of an island, so perhaps sea breezes were being accounted for?

Either way, it would be a decision to go, and the appropriate flight plan was filed and then it was back to see Ahmed. Unsurprisingly, Avgas price from a barrel was even worse than Avgas price from a bowser, but there hadn't been a choice. Soon he would be running out of dollars, but at least he'd soon be in Europe and his credit cards should be acceptable.

Having read about his destination Iraklion on SkyDemon Pilot Notes, he made sure his AOPA membership card and lanyard was around his neck – it would be needed! As would the Canadian-recommended Urine Management System that he had fitted after leaving flight briefing. With the route already in SkyDemon (but with no mapping until Crete) and in Garmin 496 he was soon cleared to taxi to 34L. With the runway being 4000m he requested to go from the crossway which would still give him 2500m and save taxying and precious fuel. This was allowed as long as he could do power checks before moving. He was then cleared to cross the eastern runway to reach 34L and take off immediately on reaching, which he did.

Gaining altitude quickly he was soon crossing the Nile again and was then over the Western Desert. 490NM in a straight line, over desert was not a particularly pleasant experience. Once past the Nile there was nothing to see, and little to think about except to make the correct changes to fuel tanks and monitor all the other instruments. Much more instrumentation than his Cessna, so at least there was more to look at, and he was actually getting used to the layout now. With all the time available, it was easy to continue checking his progress against the PLOG. Whilst SkyDemon had no mapping it still gave him distances and timing to next waypoint (as did the Garmin) and it was reassuring to see there was no stronger wind than forecast to lengthen the flight.

Before reaching the coast, he passed over the eastern edge of the Qattara Depression – an area of salt marshes shaped like a teardrop and about the size of Lake Ontario. The second lowest place in Africa it was 133m (436 feet) below sea level and were he not at such a great height he might have been able to see the cheetahs who thrive there (and perhaps their prey, gazelles) but he was flying at FL85 to comply with the semi-circular rule, and nothing is easy to spot from 9000 feet above.

It took more than four hours before the Mediterranean Sea came into view and by then he'd consumed the granola bars he'd bought from hotel fridge and taken sips of water as and when needed. As he coasted out, he reflected that although it would be nearly two hours before he reached land again, after two-thirds of that time he would be back in Europe, which was surprisingly comforting. There would still be a long way to go, but it wouldn't feel such an alien environment as Africa, and besides he'd have proper mapping on his devices and all the air traffic controllers should have acceptable English.

His concerns about fuel were unfounded as he was making better headway than planned – the wind and weather gods were being kind, and he calculated he would have an hour left in his tanks when he landed. Sure enough, after six hours from leaving Hurghada he had spoken to Athens Information on 130.925 and was "in" Europe. They passed him straight to Iraklion Radar/Approach on 123.975 who would co-ordinate his overflight of the military base at Kasteli. The Kasteli ATZ reached up to 4000 feet so he couldn't commence descent until after, and before then the mountains to his starboard were up to 7000 feet.

Just above 4000 feet as he crossed the airbase, he could see the F-16 fighters on their dispersals but also the enormous amount of construction work just to the southeast of the field. This was to be the new airport to replace Iraklion. Originally planned to be completed in 2027, the COVID pandemic had put everything back and despite having been started in 2020, it would now be 2028 at best.

Once Approach had asked how long he would be staying, he was vectored to Runway 27. Whilst he could have used the shorter 30, the intention was for him to turn off after landing and position on the eastern apron – away from the main terminal and the tourist traffic. Despite his best intentions he landed long and whilst he should easily have made the first turnoff at 570m from the threshold, he had to take the second at 800m. Wouldn't have happened if he was in his Cessna! By the time he was parking up as instructed by Kazantzakis Ground, there was a truck approaching from Skyserv-Handling Services.

Mike Gray had confirmed these were the people to use and they were expecting him. Pilot Notes on SkyDemon included tales of outrageous handling charges, but with his AOPA card on show, it was a mere 25 Euros plus fuel which they would arrange after he cleared immigration. Escorted by Skyserv, immigration went very smoothly, and Martin was happy that the forthcoming ETIAS rules hadn't come in yet. These would mean more paperwork (or electronic messaging) in advance but hopefully that was still two years away. Once he had been accepted into Europe the truck took him back to the Robin whilst it was being refuelled, and then returned him to the main terminal so he could source an hotel for the night. Thanks, Christos!

The tourist desk came up trumps with Marvel Deluxe Rooms which were less than a mile away and overlooked the coast. No single rooms but a double was only about £50 and although there was no restaurant, they served breakfast, and were surrounded by eateries (recommended was "7 Thaleses" for seafood). What wasn't to like? The taxi got him there in minutes.

By then he was feeling rather drained. Even the easy day he'd had, yesterday, had been over-ridden by the long flight – not physically all that tiring but mentally - with concerns re fuel, over water, and the thought of another long day tomorrow, but at least it wasn't to be so far. Better that he now sent Jean a mail with the latest news, and then give her a quick telephone call before going to eat. He knew that if he had a beer, or perhaps wine now he was here, he might not do his duty and call later. Whilst they were speaking an enormous cruise liner passed by the seafront and he realised he was right next to the docks. Hopefully the restaurant wouldn't be fully booked.

It wasn't quite full, and they found him a "Johnny No Mates" table in a corner where he could still watch the passing tourists while he partook of meze to start, then barbouri (red mullet) followed by honey and baklava. After all, he'd hardly eaten since breakfast. A bottle of Retsina was a fine accompaniment, but he stopped short of finishing the bottle and switched to coffee. Then it was back to his room to catch up with the news, and plan, of course.

Except he didn't do any planning. As soon as the world news was on, his eyelids started closing and knowing he wouldn't pay the best attention, he went to bed with a view to an early start.

Friday 14 April 2023

The early morning sun flooded into his room, and he didn't need the alarm that he had set on his phone. Now he was in Europe, SkyDemon gave him all he needed for planning, and he could work in the relaxed atmosphere of his hotel room before going for breakfast. Initially he'd thought of a straight line of 487NM to his Italian destination, Reggio Calabria (LICR), but having had so long over water yesterday he thought it better to not push his luck and would make doglegs to stay over land for as long as possible.

With a series of Greek islands that he could pass over or nearby he wouldn't be too far from land until he came to the last leg which meant some 250NM over water with nothing to either side. But the overall distance would be 518NM – not much more and feeling distinctly more comfortable – and less than yesterday's time above the Mediterranean. Furthermore, he was being promised a tailwind for the majority of the flight, and there was a chance he could be in the air for four hours or less.

With that thought a leisurely breakfast was in order, followed by submitting his flightplans via SkyDemon and after checkout a taxi back to Nikos Kasantzakia Airport. Checking in with Christos, he was escorted through immigration and then chauffeured out to the ramp. Once everything was loaded and he was ready, he used his hand-held transceiver to listen to the ATIS before calling Ground for engine start. As soon as he started Christos waved and departed the apron in his truck.

Despite a slight easterly wind, they were still using runway 27 so from his position on the eastern ramp it was a short taxi, once he had done power checks and received his clearance. Soon he was climbing for FL80 and heading due west towards Prases (the highest peak would be well to port, and he was good VFR) where he would turn for his first dogleg to the northwest, giving him the luxury of having been over Crete's land for 84NM before coasting out. But even the next piece of water would only be 50NM before he passed over Kithira Airport (LGKC) – all the airports had secondary names and Kithira was Alexandros Aristotelous Onassis. Even though it was a familiar name it was good that he only needed to call "Kithira Information". Once overhead Kithira it was a even shorter hop over water to reach Kalamata (LGKL - and home of the olives he favoured on Thursday night pizzas!).

Kalamata to Zakinthos (LGZA) was water too but alongside a bay to his starboard that was only 20NM away. At this height the tailwind was doing a great job. From there he coasted out for the long crossing. With nothing to look at but blue sea he concentrated on his regular checks and fuel cock changes and mused about what he'd learned about the Robin. One thing he had been warned of, was running continuously at an engine speed between 2150 and 2350 revs per minute, but that was never likely to happen as he needed 2550 to give him 65% power and a decent speed. No doubt the lower engine speed might have been used when bimbling about at home and hoping to save Avgas, but not now he was warned.

About forty minutes after passing over Zakinthos he was talking to Roma Information on 129.575 to report entering their airspace and was quickly passed to Reggio Approach on 120.275. They instructed him to keep at FL80 as he would pass over TANGO Corridor 6 – a NE/SW route for unmanned aircraft active up to 5000 feet every day. Once past that he could make a gradual descent which he commenced when land felt close enough.

The tailwind that had speeded him to the destination meant that he now had to fly past the airport to join for runway 15, but he was still touching down just on the four-hour mark. On touchdown he was asked to take the first left turn which led to the Aero Club apron which was alongside the police station. As an internal European flight there was no need for customs procedure, but they still wanted sight of passport etc.

Having been briefed by Mike Gray, he'd prepared the ground with the various participants – SACAL (the airport) took his landing fees of €6, Aviopartner charged him handling at €52 and Carboil delivered Avgas and relieved him of €3.53 per litre. All round it was expensive, but there was little choice, as so few Italian ports have Avgas. It just seemed odd that you had to make separate payments to all involved…….

The real bonus (as explained by the Aero Club) was that he could walk just a couple of hundred metres to the "B & B Airport House" which not only overlooked the runway but was opposite "400 Gradi" Pizza House. It was a no-brainer where to stay, and he was early enough to have a relaxing evening and enjoy corresponding with Jean.

Saturday 15 April 2023

When Martin awoke, he realised he was on his own. Not just in the hotel, but now the route ahead was all his. Mike Gray's job had finished once he entered Europe, and since Crete all the planning had been his and would continue the same. He'd made the right decision of going to Reggio Calabrio, as comments on the web suggested that Mike's suggested choice of Lamezia Terme was very unlikely to have any Avgas, and a call from Crete had confirmed that.

Next stop would be France after another long day, and the previous evening he had decided on Marseille Provence (LFML). Having charged all his equipment overnight, he was playing with SkyDemon on his Samsung pad to determine the best route with the news on television in the background. It was Rai TV broadcasting – in Italian of course – but from the text below the screen he could grasp what was happening. In images that were being captured on a mobile phone, his attention was caught by a Saudi Airbus A330 exploding in a ball of flames on an airport stand. Seconds later a Boeing 737 did the same and shells were raining all around the airport – which was Khartoum!

Rai's studio reporter was explaining what was being seen but the language meant little to him, yet from the text on the news ticker he gathered it was a battle going on between Sudan government forces and their own Rapid Support Forces and airliner after airliner was being destroyed. Christ! He'd only left there three days ago. This must have been what Zahid had been worried about, and why Ron Stirk had queried if he had left there.

Switching his pad from SkyDemon to the BBC News Channel it became clearer. The RSF had mobilised against the government and the whole of Khartoum was in the battle zone. The best communication was coming from the airport where 14 aircraft had already been destroyed, but other images showed tanks and troop carriers moving through the city streets which were strewn with bodies of both civilians and soldiers. At least Jean knew he was back in Europe already, but he knew that once he reached home it was likely he'd have questions about why he'd even been there. But he was safe, and he hoped Zahid would be too.

He'd learn more that evening but for now he had to plan, and the sooner he was at home, the happier they both would be. The fastest route to Marseille would be a straight-line distance of 574NM travelling northwest but that would mean at least 4.5 hours over water, and he just wasn't that brave. Better to route up through Italy then make a shorter sea crossing east to west, which is what he now planned. Only trouble was that the shortest route up the western coast would take him into Class A airspace near Rome, and neither he nor the aircraft were licensed/equipped for that. It was necessary to go further inland and that extended the overall route to 651NM. Besides which there would be some manoeuvring to avoid French restricted airspace and follow the VFR joining procedures at Provence.

Flight plan submitted, and necessary equipment fitted it was short stroll back to check out with the police and load his small amount of luggage. When he came to do the customary A-check of the aircraft he was a little perturbed that he seemed to have burned more oil than on previous legs and needed to top up with nearly two quarts. Until now, it had hardly used any, so he would need to keep an eye on that.

Clearance for start was given and he waited for the Lycoming to warm up before he did his power checks where he was and receive his clearances. Once ready, it was only a 100m taxi to the runway where he turned right into 33 – the wind had changed since yesterday. The aero club had been at the midpoint of the 2058m runway, so there was ample left for him to simply turn into the runway and be cleared to take off.

He was already heading in the right direction for his first turning point of Salerno (LIRI) and although he would be over water enroute for over an hour, effectively he was flying from the toe of Italy's boot towards the ankle, so would never be far from the arch of the foot. The furthest he would be away from land on that leg would be 40NM, and at his cruising height of FL80 he would be one and a half miles high so the westerly wind would almost blow him to the shore if he adopted the best glide speed immediately, were he to have a total engine failure. It was more comforting than the last leg which would be with a two-hour water crossing, but at least some of that time would be in reaching range of Corsica.

Martin was getting used the boredom with nothing to see below him, but at least he could see the coast which gave confidence. As usual he maintained his regular FREDA checks, but he would also think about the trip to date. Putting Khartoum to one side, it had all gone rather well, and he calculated that he was approaching 35 hours flying so far – more than many a private pilot flies in a full year, and he'd done it in eight days.

As he overflew Salerno, he could see the construction work far below him. The airport had been shut since 2016 but was being rebuilt to launch as the new Amalfi Coast destination due to open in July 2024. No doubt Ryanair and/or EasyJet would take advantage. Turning onto a heading of 320 degrees magnetic he now tracked inside Italy's western coast which was scattered with available airports and aerodromes if necessary. Safety height was 7900 feet so FL80 worked well, and he'd filed as an IFR flight with his next turning point at Pontecagnano. This would keep him clear of not just the Rome airspace but the many restricted and danger areas to the west.

With mountains reaching up towards him it was important to keep to his planned height and watch out for any mountain wave effect – but the relatively light winds and the forecast didn't suggest such. The Robin sat there happily, Lycoming purring contentedly, but it would have been even easier with a wing-leveller or even an autopilot (not that he would have known how to use either without training). It was a shame he had to move inland, because he had hoped to pass over Lake Bracciano. Next to the southwest edge of the lake at Vigna di Valle there were the hangars of the Italian Air Force Museum – there were four large aircraft outside in the open, and more than 60 aircraft inside he had read – he'd decided it would make a good visit if ever nearby again.

There was nothing at Pontecagnano except for the Monte Cosce – a peak at 3,678 feet, but it had been the turning point that worked for the restrictions and was plotted in SkyDemon which made it so easy. Turning there, another 73NM and he reached his next point of Grosetto (LIRS) which had a convenient VOR (GRO) on the airport. He'd been cleared through by Approach and informed them as he turned overhead onto a westerly heading, and almost directly into the headwind. Just what he didn't need over the water. Only fifteen minutes later and he was above the northern tip of an island which turned out to be Elba. Martin's brain flashed back to his first holiday with Jean. They had gone to Elba with a Court Line package holiday that cost all of £30 for both flight, ferry and hotel. Flying pastel-coloured BAC 1-11s, Court Line brought affordable holidays to the masses, and they had taken advantage shortly after becoming engaged, which had been a pre-requisite of Jean being allowed to go.

Just before he reached the northern tip of Corsica, he had entered French Airspace. On his flight plan he had entered Flight Rules as "Y" indicating commencement as IFR and finishing as VFR, then in Item 15 he had entered the Marseille FIR boundary as the change point. This would be important for his airport fees at Marseille Provence. Corsica soon passed below and then it was another hour of nothing but water until he coasted in at Saint-Tropez aiming for the Microlight field "Club Ulm de Thèmes". Once he had site of the coast he had been gradually descending as he would need to be at 3500 feet (above a restricted area) and shortly afterwards below 3000 feet (below another restriction). The route toward the micro field kept him away from all the red-hatched areas denoting danger or restricted areas to the south as shown on SkyDemon.

Having made the transit of Class D airspace and talking to Nice they were soon glad to hand him to Provence Approach who instructed entry from Point SC (1 NM west of Cap Croisette), then progressively route Point S, Point SA, and towards Point SB before being allowed to join left base for runway 31R. No doubt it would have been simpler to make an IFR arrival and use the localiser MPV, but it would have impacted his arrival fees considerably – and it was going to be expensive enough already.

Down to the maximum height of 1500 feet, he confirmed VFR and quoted the ATIS pressure setting and received onward clearance to join for 31R. On touchdown he rolled to after the midpoint of the 3440m runway and turned off onto taxiway G1 to reach the General Aviation Area. After closing down and with everything switched off, his first job was to exit the aircraft and open the stopcock on his urine management system out of sight of the officials that would no doubt approach him soon. The kit had been a godsend, and hopefully would only be needed once more.

He was just starting to chill and get his flight bag and luggage out of the Robin when the Gendarmerie and Customs arrived. Polite enough, they explained that a South African registered light aircraft was unusual to say the least, and they believed a ramp check was in order. Oh god, this was going to be a long day……

Wishing to keep the mood light, he explained the reason for his flights and how the wonderful French-built machine would be much more appreciated in UK where there were lots of Robins, than in South Africa – and he was effectively bringing her home. That was understood, but the 53-item checklist still came out to be completed. The days he had spent preparing his folder with all the necessary documentation paid off, with everything filed in the order he knew would be asked, by about item 30 they were getting bored – it was obvious he knew what was required and they were unlikely to find any omissions, and many of the remaining items wouldn't apply as they only referred to commercial aircraft and flights.

With that, it was a quick look at the contents of the aircraft and a check of his luggage and flight bag - which were both too small to conceal much - and he was allowed to walk into the GA Terminal to have his passport stamped there. Again, his handling agent would be Aviapartner and he registered at their desk but had had enough and decided to refuel and pay fees etc in the morning. The Ibis Marseille Provence Airport hotel was a few metres walk away and as an Accor Hotels member, he'd earn discount and points. A beer was calling.

Sunday 16 April 2023

The previous night had been full of revelations. The first was that unusually, a French hotel had BBC World Service amongst the available TV channels, and he had learnt more about Khartoum and the increasing body count. He'd seen pictures of burnt-out Ilyushin and Antonov freighters as well as fighter aircraft and attack helicopters. The realisation of what had happened and what might have happened struck home, and he made time to email Ron Stirk and thank him again for his concern and let him know of progress, when he would reach UK, and how well the Robin was performing. He did mention the extra oil usage as the engineer might offer any thoughts or tips – and it reminded him to have another close look in the morning. He didn't hear back.

The second revelation was a personal one. He realised he was in familiar territory at last, having flown in France many times, and that the next leg had no need to be so onerous. He'd need to have his passport stamped as he exited, or could be in trouble next time he came, so had planned to fly the 450NM or so to Le Touquet, a regular destination and leave France from there. But realisation dawned that it would be an internal flight and whilst planning was important, no filing of flight plan would be necessary. Moreover, he didn't need to do it in one hop, and could take a comfort break at somewhere enroute.

He also realised just how much he was missing Jean and home. It had been a great adventure (not quite over yet) but he was tired. A younger man would have relished the long hours more, and although he had enjoyed the experience, it would never be repeated – that was a promise to himself.

That decision made, he'd had a good night's sleep and awoke early to another surprise. It was raining. More than a week of flying through almost cloudless skies had come to an end. What was worrying was that his restricted instrument qualification, an

IR(R), would not allow flight in cloud in France – it was just a UK privilege. At least he had good resources to obtain weather information and that would add to the planning task, whereas he'd hardly had to consider until now. The French rules meant that he *could* fly VFR on top of clouds, but to be legal he had to climb and descend through gaps, so if the forecast for his destination was more than 4 Oktas coverage it was probably a non-starter, and besides he needed to get up through a hole first.

The forecast looked more promising. Despite the rain, the visibility at Marseille was within limits, and the overcast was at 2200 feet. Further north the base was higher, so perhaps the local weather was due to being on the coast. A good plan would take him low-level to the airfield at Uzes (LFNU) and whilst SkyDemon showed a minimum safety altitude of 2400 feet, that was for IFR, and as VFR he would be safe at 1900 feet. The only obstacle shown on the chart was a mast 900 feet above ground level, but then he realised after Uzes he would need to climb to above the Cevennes and then Massif Central, with no guarantee of the cloud base there. He'd decided to try to get to Chartres, but being VFR could land elsewhere if necessary and the weather closed him down.

The plan became to route towards Uzes but once south of Avignon, turn north and keep going through Avignon Caumont and Valence Chabeuil before reaching Lyon Saint Exupery and turning for Chartres. The highest safety altitude on the northern leg was between Avignon (LFMV) and Valence (LFLU) where 3500 feet was necessary, but the local TAFs suggested that was achievable by the time he would reach there.

If it all worked, he could be in Chartres in less than three hours. There was still Avgas in his tanks, and he could afford to only take on a further 100 litres at Marseille – an excellent result as they were to charge €4 per litre! He'd been to Chartres the previous year in the company of Bob Bailey, and it was a friendly field with low costs (and a fabulous cathedral – the reason for the previous trip).

Planning done and continental breakfast consumed, it was a stroll back to the airport and he didn't need to fit "the equipment" as he could drop into anywhere if he felt the need. Aviapartner obliged with fuel and relieved him of large numbers of Euros for that and the importantly *VFR* landing and handling. Whilst they had been fuelling, the rain reduced until it was just "spotting" and the skies began to brighten. Perhaps a more direct route would have been possible, but a plan is a plan!

The walk round the aircraft had confirmed no more great oil loss, so he relaxed somewhat. ATIS provided the information he needed – they were using runway 13 - and before start he called Provence Prévol on 121.730 for clearances. Power checks were done where he was parked and then it was short taxi back to the threshold and he was gone. Poorer than when he arrived but pleased to be going home via familiar territory…….

He was still low-level as he turned north at Mouriès, and then was a series of Class D airspaces he needed to cross but the local ATCOs cleared him through. All the while the cloud base was lifting, and the forecast was coming good. Whilst tracking to Lyon he passed over six sites which were marked as aerobatic areas but there was no sign of activity. France seems to have dozens of these areas but whenever he'd visited, he had never seen one in use.

Shortly after turning overhead Lyon, he reached his ideal cruising height of FL60. He was below the (now) high overcast but at enough altitude to avoid the restricted areas that would be below him during the 219NM leg (there were a couple that reached up to 3700 feet). The Robin purred along comfortably whilst he snacked on the confectionary from the Ibis mini-bar, and in what seemed a short time (compared to previous flights) he neared his destination, and the magnificent cathedral came into view.

No one was answering his radio calls, so he gave blind calls and as he approached runway 09 the cathedral was to his right. He was soon rolling to the end and turning left to reach the parking area in front of the club. As he'd discovered on the last trip, there were no landing fee, and it was necessary to have a Total card to obtain fuel – but the bonus was it was only €2.99 per litre. Despite no-one on the radio, a gentleman emerged from the clubhouse and welcomed him in. A rather one-sided conversation ensued due to language difficulties, but coffee was offered and accepted.

Soon he was airborne again. It was less than an hour to Le Touquet (LFAT) and on reaching he was going to consider whether to make the final push and get home, but he'd decide once he got there. The beauty of routing to Chartres was that he could avoid the Paris airspace as he had done on the previous trip. A straight line took him to the entry point for Le Touquet at Point Sierra. Since leaving Chartres nobody had wanted to talk to him and that suited him just fine, but he announced his presence to Le Touquet as he passed Abbeville.

They were using runway 13 so it was necessary to pass overhead and join downwind for a left-hand circuit, going out over the sea for a short time, and extending the downwind leg somewhat to allow traffic already on final to land. Once parked it was into the terminal to decide what to do.

The decision was easy. As much as he wanted to be home, the weather would not allow it. Whilst Le Touquet was relatively clear, METARs for Lydd and Southend showed the cloud nearly down to the ground, and at Biggin (a similar height to Rochester) it was unflyable. Using his IR(R) he would have been legal to attempt an approach at either Lydd or Southend, but if he did manage a cloud break in time, what then? Lydd is the back of nowhere and no nearby accommodation, and Southend has a Holiday Inn, but then he still wouldn't reach Rochester until the next day – and that assumed the weather would break. The long TAF for Gatwick and the pressure chart suggested that morning would be better, so the die was cast.

It would have been nice to go into Le Touquet town and eat at Pérard his favourite seafood restaurant, but hotel prices were high, and it was too far to walk with bag and flight bag, so the obvious answer was the Mercure Le Touquet – again part of the Accor Group so discounted to Martin and only a 600 metre walk from the airport parking lot. Not the cheapest in the area, but convenience outweighed everything else. An online reservation assured him of room and discount, and after paying his landing fee of €36, he set off.

Monday 17 April 2023

On Sunday evening, Jean had been happy to learn that he was so close but sorry he couldn't have made that final hop. Nevertheless, if he let her know forecast arrival time, she would be at Rochester to greet him and take him home in her SLC.

Martin hadn't estimated a time and would let her know today, as first he needed to check the weather, and then speak to Rochester to ensure it wasn't waterlogged and closed. It was April and it shouldn't be, but stranger things have happened, and he'd been away a long time. The news was good on both counts, so it was a very simple flight plan to be submitted along with a GAR submission for Border Force.

Flight time would be just over half an hour and whilst he only needed to be above 1500 feet to avoid the restricted areas where drones were searching the Channel for migrants, he would climb high enough to be able to glide to land if necessary. SkyDemon would draw a circle around his aircraft image to show his gliding range. FL60 would probably do the job and then approaching land he could commence descent to below the London TMA. The GAR had to be submitted at least two hours before departure, so as soon as he had spoken to Rochester and Kelvin had confirmed they were open, it was submitted, and Jean was texted with the noon arrival time. It was nearly over.

Back at the airport there was no need for fuel, so just a matter of getting his passport stamped as he exited, the usual A-check, and he was on his way. Shortly after take-off he went straight to Lydd Approach and confirmed his estimate for the FIR, and although he couldn't see it, SkyDemon detected one of the drones working ahead and below. Soon the white cliffs were below him and he was already in the descent. Everything looked so familiar, he could almost feel himself relaxing – nothing like home territory to be comfortable. He couldn't resist a minor diversion over his house to check that Jean was on her way. Yes, the SLC was gone, and his Jaguar was in its normal place.

Once past Ashford, he had switched to Rochester on 122.255 and just listened for now, but when east of the airfield he called. Nigel was the duty AFISO and was surprised to hear a Zulu Sierra registration calling up, but thought he recognised the pilot's voice. Kelvin obviously hadn't mentioned anything to him, as when told it was inbound, he asked how long he would be staying, for parking purposes. "It's Martin, Nigel. I'll be here for a few days before taking it to Thurrock for maintenance and re-registration. Kelvin has found me a temporary space in hangar three".

With that he joined dead-side for 20, and after a rather longer circuit than he'd need in the Cessna, made a pretty reasonable landing. As he taxied between the old and new control towers, there was a mob (of at least six) Border Force officials waiting at the gate. Since Air Search had taught them things, they seemed to be there more and more often!

Fortunately, the lead member recognised Martin from previous discussions about where things might be hidden in light aircraft and after a quick chat, John and Ryan were allowed to put the aircraft safely away in the hangar, whilst he walked to the car park to meet Jean. They were at home in twenty-five minutes, and a real cup of tea was required, but first, Louis the Westie needed to calm down. He did eventually – and then curled up and went to sleep, which Martin thought was probably a good idea.

But the flying isn't over until the logbooks are done! Whilst he'd filled in the journey logbook each day, which was necessary in case of a ramp check, he hadn't risked taking his personal logbook, and that needed completion as did the airframe and engine logbooks. It made sense to do it now, because once he really relaxed and perhaps had a glass, he knew it would be an early night. Job done, he sank into the sofa and was asleep in minutes.

Tuesday 18 April 2023

There is no rest for the wicked, and Martin was awoken by Louis banging on the office door (where he slept), wanting to be let out. It was only 06.30 – it was like he'd never been away. With Louis happily keeping guard behind the driveway gate, Martin made his first cup of tea of the day and returned to the sofa.

Last night, he'd managed to finish the logbooks but hadn't totted anything up until now. Jean would be rising soon, but meanwhile he calculated that in 10 days, he had flown 5,730NM (6589 statute miles). The aircraft had logged 44 hours flying time (airframe and engine only record time in the air, not taxying) whilst he had logged 46 hours of being in charge. It was nearly half of his normal annual flying time.

He would have started assessing total costs of getting home, but even though he knew how much cash he'd expended (which was nearly all the dollars he had taken), it was best to wait for credit card statements that would show what the foreign currency exchange rates had been and what had translated into sterling. Besides, he wouldn't know total costs until Ian had prepared a new Certificate of Airworthiness and put the Robin on the UK register.

Despite that, he now had an aircraft to prepare for sale and started to trawl through the various sellers' adverts online, to find price comparisons, and began to be thoroughly disappointed. There were just a few Robins for sale, and they looked cheap. Not what he had expected at all, and many had "price reduced" stickers emblazoned across the advert. Conversely, the regular Pipers and Cessnas were looking over-priced, which wasn't surprising considering what new aircraft now cost.

As soon as it was working hours, he called David Morris at Just Plane Trading for an opinion. David was a straight dealer who was happy to buy anything at the right price and always managed to resell, and his opinion would be valuable – besides which he had two Robins on his books, which also looked cheap. "Since Robin went into the equivalent of Chapter 11 prices everywhere have dropped. And if yours is one of those in the AD it will be unsellable until it's sorted". Good grief, he'd missed something!

As soon as off the phone he started searching the web. On 27 February Robin Aircraft had gone into a "protection arrangement" to safeguard the company – equivalent to the USA Chapter 11 which protects companies from their debtors whilst restructuring. The problem had been caused by poor manufacture of wing spars with examples of delamination of the wooden structure. On 7 March EASA had issued an Airworthiness Directive (2023-0048-E) restricting flights by certain serials numbers to flying "carefully", not exceeding 60 degrees of bank, and limiting maximum speed to 124 knots. He'd just flown all the way from Africa at 130 knots!

Normally he was up to speed on anything happening in aviation, hearing good and bad news through not just official sources like the CAA SkyWise, but from Flyer Magazine whose online news and livestreams covered nearly all anyone could need – well worth his membership and that included free landing vouchers each month. The realisation dawned on him – it had all been happening when he was in the bush at Mabula. Robin's business troubles would have started whilst he was preparing to leave for South Africa, and he must have been making an offer to the crooked lawyer just as the AD was issued. Damn.

Fortunately, examination of the AD showed that his Robin was too old to have the problem, as it was a 1500 series production number from 1981, whereas the potentially faulty aircraft were 2100 series from 1992 and later. Phew! But the demise of Robin was bound to affect spares and prices. This was a matter he wouldn't share with Jean until he'd thought about it.

No matter what the Robin was now worth, he'd still need to sell as soon as possible as his savings had been used and he needed them back. He'd never had a lot of money, but he had a reasonable nest-egg in reserve for any needs that might occur. There had been enough for zero-timing the Cessna engine if and when it needed it, so it was important to move the Robin on. Furthermore, there would be a VAT liability when it was re-registered. At this moment it hadn't been declared as an import, and he was counting on the 180-day exemption for aircraft coming into the UK from outside the EU, but on registration it would be evident it was here to stay. On entry to the workshop, he'd begin the importation process. As a private individual he had no means of reclaiming the VAT, but it would add to the value he could sell for.

A call to Ian at Thurrock determined that he would be happy to do both certification and re-registration, but the workshop was full and perhaps it would be two weeks before he could look at it. He'd have to wait his turn, as he trusted Ian to do a good job at the right price. Until the work was done there was no point starting to advertise, so he would spend the next few days catching up with domestic duties and gaining some quality time with Jean and Louis.

Lesson learnt; he watched the Flyer Livestreams on YouTube that he had missed and made sure he was up to date on aviation knowledge. The news from Khartoum was getting worse and there were now 20 aircraft wrecked or damaged – but they were only machines - and the death toll was rising dramatically. The UK government was planning to send troops to guard evacuees and RAF aircraft which would be used to bring British Nationals home. In other news, the country was gearing up for the coronation of Charles and Camilla.

Friday 21 April 2023

By logging into the various credit card accounts he had used, he could now see the values his payments had been exchanged to, and now had the full costs (prior to Ian's work and import VAT). The one good thing was that the crooked lawyer's invoice was lower than it should have been, so VAT liability would be reduced proportionally. Despite that, the total wasn't pretty.

Moreover, Kelvin had only been expecting to find him space in the hangar for a few days, whilst another aircraft was away for maintenance, whereas Ian couldn't help for another fortnight. He could have taken it to Thurrock, but it wouldn't be good to leave it outside as he had no covers, and English weather is not good to wood and fabric aeroplanes.

After discussion with Kelvin, it made sense to move the Cessna out of hangar five and tie it down outside – he had a Cambrai cover for that which had recently been renovated and reproofed, so it would do no real harm for a couple of weeks. Longer term it might have to stay there if he couldn't sell the Robin quickly and there was no more hangar space at Rochester. The Robin could then occupy his prime space in the new hangar.

With that intention in mind, he rolled up at the airport, to be greeted by Colin, who often flew with him, and was the nearest thing to an aircraft spotter he could be, without admitting it – he would record and photograph anything he hadn't seen before. "There's a South African registered Robin Regent in the main hangar!" he declared. Martin had to admit that he already knew and explained. No-one had been told of his plans just in case it didn't come off and that way he wouldn't have been embarrassed.

Now that he knew, no doubt Colin was already wondering whether he'd get a ride in the new aircraft – he logged all his passenger flights and had amassed more than 1000 hours – of which many hundred had been with Martin. But as they chatted, John and Ryan from the fire crew approached and informed Martin that his engineer had just arrived a few minutes ago and was working on the undercarriage already. "Who? What?" Why would Ian be here when he would take the aircraft to Thurrock? And there was nothing wrong with the undercarriage as far as he knew. "No, it's not Ian – he sounds South African – said something about the spat repair. He's under the aircraft now."

"Come with me guys, this isn't right, and I need to know what's going on". The Robin had been put at the back of the hangar as it wasn't to be used. In front of it was Rob Taylor's Arrow and Rob was just finishing polishing it – probably a weekly occurrence. Beneath the Robin's port wing a pair of overalled legs were sticking out, and a roll of spanners and screwdrivers was unfurled and lying next to them.

"Hello. Can we talk?" The overalls slid out from beneath the wing and stood up. It was Ron Stirk. "What on earth…..?".

"Howzit? can we speak privately?" said Ron "I need to discuss something with you". Martin's mind was racing. If there was something wrong with the aircraft that Ron knew about, why would he not have said something at Wonderboom? And why didn't he fix it? And why fly all the way to UK and arrive unannounced? There had to be more going on…..

"John, would you two and Rob give us some space but don't go too far? I might need your help". Ron was a typical big South African and if they were about to have a serious fall out, Martin might feel a little lonely.

Once his friends were outside the hangar Ron came clean. His concern for Martin and the aircraft wasn't what it appeared to be. He knew full well what Glen Meyburgh used his Robin for. The raiders who had killed him knew he bought stolen diamonds, but not that once a month he flew them to Harare to his accomplices. Once out of South Africa they could be fenced on. Ron did know, because he had installed the new inspection hatches under the wing that had no necessary engineering purpose. But they did allow access and an easy way to attach a small bag to one of the wing ribs. Payment for his work on the Robin was always in cash and more than he asked for – it was their agreement.

Ron had counted on there being a consignment inside the Robin, and when he'd done the export CoA for Martin, he'd found it. But inside South Africa it had little value. The Kimberley Process is a way a certificating rough diamonds and showing origins to allow them to change country. The stolen diamonds would have no certification and could not be sold at true value inside South Africa, but once they reached Zimbabwe they could be polished, and false receipts created. Which would explain why the lawyer had had an enquiry from Harare – no doubt from Glen's associates in crime. De Klerk, the lawyer, would have known nothing of this but just wanted to line his pockets, and the Zimbabweans would not have known he was corrupt.

"So, the best thing was to let you export the package. Now it's here we can maximise the value from contacts we have been given at Hatton Garden – you and I just have to come to the right arrangement".

Martin played along. "Show me!". Beneath the port wing they looked up and Ron snipped off the tie-wraps attached to the rib and the pouch fell out. If they hadn't arrived when they did, Ron could have been long gone, very quickly. Martin swept up the pouch with his hand before Ron had chance to do the same and rolled out from under the wing. Standing quickly, he thrust the pouch into his pocket and called his friends back. "Rob, please can you dial 999 and get the police here? Tell them we have detained a smuggler, and he may be dangerous. Stand still Ron – you are going nowhere!" At that, John and Ryan picked up an aircraft towbar each from near the hangar door and were shortly rejoined by Rob when he'd made the call. John used his airport walkie-talkie to inform that tower what was happening, and they were quickly joined by Kelvin and John Price who happened to have been in the tower. Nigel would remain up there manning the radio.

"Ron, you weren't to know that there is no way I could come to any arrangement. Now just wait there quietly – there are six of us now". There wasn't any point of him trying anything. He'd been dropped at the airport by taxi so had no means of escape, and didn't know the surrounding area anyway, so where would he run to?

Kent's finest arrived rapidly, mob-handed in four cars. Perhaps thinking it was migrants running amok at the airport, there were twelve officers including an ARV crew. Kelvin fetched them from car park to hangar and Martin started the story. The sergeant having heard enough, Ron was arrested for conspiracy to smuggle, and he and Martin were taken to Police HQ in Sutton Road, Maidstone for further questioning. Meanwhile the Robin was being surrounded by tape proclaiming "POLICE LINE DO NOT CROSS". Good job it was at the back of the hangar, thought John and Ryan.

In Custody

It was obvious to the interrogators that Martin was on the side of the good. His story made sense and he had been responsible for the detention of Ron. Besides, apart from being a member of Air Search, he was a police volunteer and known to both Tim Smith, the new Chief Constable, and Matthew Scott, the PCC.

The pouch was emptied onto the desk between them all, and the contents looked distinctly unremarkable. There were twenty-three stones, dull-looking, rough, and nothing like one would think of as a diamond, but there was no doubt what they were due to the cubic shapes. With the explanation (albeit hearsay) that the stones would have been bought from individuals who had stolen them from the De Beers' mine, they were bagged up as stolen property.

Whilst Ron had not been involved in their theft, nor taking part in their transportation, he had facilitated the same by modifying the Robin, and therefore was party to conspiracy, and potentially receiving stolen goods had he been able to remove them. He would be held until discussions were had with South African police as to whether they should deal with him.

Martin was free to go but instructed not to touch the Robin until given leave to do so. He hoped it wouldn't be too long and said the same. He was given a lift back to the airport by the SOCO (Scenes of Crime Officer) who was sent to photograph the still open inspection hatches and gather any other evidence. Having watched that happen, there was nothing left for Martin to do except drive home and tell Jean what was happening. It wasn't going to be an easy discussion.

Waiting

There was simply no choice but to await news from Kent Police. He busied himself with discovering necessary paperwork he'd need for the importation process once he made it official, and kept Ian informed of the delay. Kelvin also had no choice – he couldn't move the Robin whilst the tape was around it and if the aircraft on maintenance came back and needed the space, Martin would have to give up the Cessna's spot in the newer hangar.

The days dragged by and were interrupted two days after the incident by the country-wide trial of an Emergency Alert being sent to nearly all the cellular phones in the country. Having been away, Martin had no prior knowledge (whereas most people knew it was coming) and he was immediately trying to contact Jean who had gone shopping. Apparently, dozens of phones were sounded off all around Sainsburys, but she had been expecting it – just had forgotten to mention to her spouse!

By 26 April the first evacuation flights were arriving from the Sudan. Royal Air Force A400s were using an airstrip at Wadi Saeedna, to the west of Khartoum, to bring British passport-holders home, whilst other refugees were making their way to the coast trying to reach Cyprus. There would have been no help for Zahid.

Meanwhile the rest of the country was gearing up for the coronation of King Charles III. President Biden had been the first head of state to visit the new king a few weeks previously and Martin was grateful he hadn't been around as it would have restricted flying – as it always does when Air Force One visits.

Eventually the law-enforcers decided there was nothing to be gained by detaining the Robin any longer, as Ron had told the full story as he knew it, and they had the pictures and evidence. They would decide on his future later. With that, Martin could take the Robin to Thurrock to start the process. Whilst Ian was more used to metal aircraft, fabric and wood were within his skill set and the DR400 was in really good condition. Engine and instruments were just like anything else, so he could soon sign it off and await the CAA providing the paperwork.

Not wanting any more expense than necessary, Martin was happy to take whatever the next in-sequence G-reg was available – besides he hoped to be selling it on so if the next owner wanted something more personal, they could pay for it. And now registrations were beginning with G-C it would make it look more modern in the adverts he would create.

All these delays had given Martin enough time to register a company and gain VAT registration too. Rather than just have to pay the VAT on import, he would be able to reclaim it along with the VAT element of Ian's bills plus the Rochester hangarage costs. Somehow, he had to make this work, and the Robin prices were not yet recovering. OK – so he would have to offer the Robin's price as "plus VAT" but if it were bought by another company, they could offset that too.

But now the flying season had started again and rather than sit around there were opportunities to fly to events in the Cessna, which he did. RAF Abingdon Airshow was a treat in May as was yet another visit to Brooklands Museum, where Mercedes allowed an elite few to land on the remaining 400m of the old runway. It took some doing, but he managed to blag his way into the Midlands Air Festival at Ragley Hall where some exhibitors land in the grounds of the stately home. He was the only visitor allowed in. If you don't ask, you don't get.

June 2023

By the end of the month the CAA had done its stuff, and the Robin with its newly painted registration was in hangar five. Martin had insured it with Visicover for the sum he thought it was worth plus a little more to be safe. The Cessna, clad in its refurbished cover, was tied down outside, and the police called Martin to Sutton Road again to tell him some news.

After discussion with the South African Police Service, it was felt better that Stirk was dealt with on home territory. In UK he had no assets that could be seized and if jailed he would simply be a cost burden on Britain, but at home SAPS could take him to task and his assets if necessary. He'd been returned under escort – nice job for whoever accompanied him!

The diamonds were to be returned to De Beers as they would have been the original owners. Having been sent pictures showing size and weights, they had given a rough estimate of value. The minimum for each would be US$3000 and the larger ones could be up to US$5000 dependant on how they could be cut and what colour and clarity they would have and were there any inclusions.

If it were the lower figure, the value of the haul would be the price he might achieve for the Robin now, and if the higher figure it would be the value he had been hoping to achieve before he knew of Robin's difficulties. But that was irrelevant – they weren't his, and he'd done everything right. De Beers thought so too and were sending a courier to collect their property and had requested a meeting with Martin.

July 2023

With June's Guernsey Air Rally out of the way, Martin had started advertising the Robin, but against the background of the French financial difficulties nobody was making overtures. He'd shuffled savings to cover his debts and VAT liabilities and had commenced to draw down a pension to make up for some of the shortfall.

There was a whole series of events lined up for the summer and he did not want to miss any due lack of funds but was getting worried. Flying trips were becoming shorter by necessity as Avgas prices continued to rise. And then the day after returning from Heveningham Hall, he received a call from the De Beers courier, who suggested they meet for lunch - and could he bring his wife and was there a good restaurant local to their home?

It was a yes on all counts and they could meet tomorrow at Reads Restaurant, Macknade Manor, Faversham. Glad that they were appropriately dressed, Jean and Martin were pleased to meet Frank Eckard, a rather young but dapper representative of De Beers. Over a very enjoyable lunch – which commenced by Frank stating that the bill would be his – they learnt all about the history of De Beers, and why they were the best diamond producers in the world. Frank also imparted the knowledge that the diamonds he had just recovered from the police would be worth far more than the estimate the police had been given, once cut, polished and appropriately graded by De Beers skilled staff.

In exchange, Martin recounted the story as he knew it, about Glen Meyburgh and what happened to him. Frank explained that they knew of their losses via employees on a regular basis and how the rough stones would be bought for next to nothing by pawn shops – indeed De Beers themselves would also visit such shops in the vicinity and buy back said stolen property with no questions asked. The pawnbroker would make a small profit, and De Beers would be able to keep the price of stones high.

Meyburgh must have been offering over the odds as he could take his profit from Zimbabwe.

For that reason, having recovered such a handsome package from Martin's aircraft they were happy to pay an appropriate reward, and would the couple like to receive it here in UK or accept an invitation to the South African Head Office to collect it?

"That's very kind, and we'd be delighted to accept, but I think I've seen enough of Africa this year, so here would be fine. I'm sure Jean would be very interested in visiting next time we are in Gauteng, but I fear it would be expensive for me once she saw the finished products!".

Frank understood, he'd heard the story of the journey back and was somewhat amazed. Like Martin and Jean, for that distance he much preferred the 787 Dreamliner. "If you can let me have your bank details, before I leave tomorrow, I'll arrange a transfer and I don't believe you will be disappointed". Details given, Reads were asked to call a cab for his return to his hotel at Heathrow, and on its arrival, they shook hands and he departed. Wow.

Good Morning!

It really was. Two days later the Rands had translated into GBP and were sitting in their joint account. The value was such that it would make up the difference between what he could probably now achieve for the Robin and what he had previously hoped for. There was still no interest being shown in the aircraft, but at least many of the expenses were now covered and liquidity had returned.

Much as he liked his new aircraft, he didn't want to fly it much because it would only add hours to the airframe and engine, so it was decided to simply fly Lycoming's recommended minimum of one hour per calendar month to keep the engine in good condition – until it was sold, and hopefully that wouldn't take six months or he'd be paying for another 50-hour/six-month check.

Besides, he enjoyed flying the Cessna more. If nothing else it was the familiarity of an aircraft he'd owned for 37 years, that meant he was totally relaxed in the machine. With that thought, he organised renewal of his IR(R) rating with John Eburne at Wellesbourne Mountford and also made his regular round of aviation events as they popped up. But in between flying days, his friends Ron Armitage and Sandra Davis from Air Search had asked him to join their entry to Pooleys Dawn to Dusk Competition, knowing the Cessna would be the ideal aircraft. The entry was to be based around the survey they had done for Border Force and Counterterrorism and would involve orbiting and photographing 91 defunct airfield sites in Kent and flying over the 54 current sites in the county that they had already photographed.

Planning would be extraordinarily complicated, and Martin would do it. Ron would provide all the research into defunct airfields, and Sandra would be both photographer and collator of the information for the needed log presentation. It took weeks for them all to prepare and on 19 August they took to the air at 07.33 to fly for more than six hours in a day. Spookily, Martin was confident that he could do it.

Following the four flights necessary, they had more weeks of work to create the log and assemble the photography and have the whole thing published privately in book form so they could submit it to the judges. It would not be until February 2024 that they would learn they had won the Pooley Sword for the best presented log.

In September, the Air Search team were surprised with an invitation to attend the Counterterrorism awards where 10 of them were awarded Certificates of Merit for their work on the airfield survey. It was all a good distraction from the fact that the Robin was incurring hangarage and insurance fees – at least by being in the new hangar it was protected and kept clean.

Nearing the End

October brought a derisory offer for the Robin, instantly refused. Various tyre-kickers had been to see it with no offers made, but this one had come from an individual who had visited and viewed twice but was disliked immediately by Martin. Whilst making a profit was important, Martin would have been prepared to take a lesser amount from an individual he liked just to clear the books, but that just wasn't the case – he neither liked the man nor his offer which would have meant a loss.

As the flying season began to tail off, Martin began to think that it would be spring before he had another chance to sell and needed to do something to keep himself occupied. He'd previously published a couple of books, one a novella and another a memoir and both had been well-received by the aviation community – and whilst there was no real money to be made, he decided to commit the trials and tribulations of his Robin adventure to paper, whilst hoping something would come up.

He was still writing when it did. After three attempted and failed takeovers, on 20 November Robin Aircraft were liquidated on the order of the French Court. Resigned to the fact that he would make a loss he considered hiring out the aircraft, but realism struck home – it would be winter soon, and the flying season was drawing to a close.

But on 1 December CEAPR (Centre-Est Aéronautique Pierre Robin) who owned the land and buildings at Darois, and also held the type certificates and design approvals, for both Robin and CAP aircraft, re-hired approximately half of the redundant Robin workers and went back into production. Different from the liquidated "Robin Aircraft" they had been established for sixty years and had bought the rights when another company, Apex Aviation, had failed in 2008.

By the end of December, the UK agent, Mistral Aviation, said they were accepting orders for new aircraft with an expected delivery time of a year.

Prices were bound to be higher and just as the USA producers' prices were rocketing (a new, basic Cessna 172 without autopilot would cost £500,000 in UK), suddenly the market for used Robins bounced back. Robin enthusiasts and owners were delighted. None more so than Martin, who by February had achieved a sale at a higher price than he had originally hoped for – after all, his machine was outside the AD range, whereas more modern aircraft would have to wait to have their spars rebuilt.

Eventually the book was finished, and when questioned by readers if he would ever do something similar his answer was always the same. "Not bloody likely!". He admitted that he was richer for both the experience gained and the cash, but his biggest pleasure had been when Jean had forgiven him for ever getting involved.

Last Word

Thank you for reading The African Robin. I hope you have enjoyed reading it, as much as I did writing it and recalling my experiences. If you have any questions, or would like to contact me, please email me at airsearch2@outlook.com.

And if you have enjoyed it, please consider leaving a two-sentence review on Amazon. Amazon reviews are what makes the world go round for writers!

Also by Martin Leusby

The aviation thriller "**The Airborne Ghost**" is 20,000 words – a novella which is 85% true and tells the story of a British private pilot visiting Paris - where he sees something that results in an airborne pursuit across Europe and puts him in a life-threatening situation.

Written for other pilots, who will understand the technicalities of both the detective work and the journey, it will be appreciated by anyone with an aviation interest who enjoys a real page-turner!

The memoir "**Pilots Progress – the highs and lows of a single-engine pilot**" is a record of how the author only ever wanted to be a pilot and his subsequent journey and flying history, told in a relaxed style and with many amusing moments.

Both books are available from Amazon in Kindle, Paperback or Hardback.

GLOSSARY

ADSB transponder radio equipment to identify aircraft to ATC and other aircraft with similar equipment

Air Search a voluntary organisation of pilots and observers who donate their flying time and costs to the resilience and emergency services

Annual once yearly aircraft inspection and maintenance

AOPA Aircraft Owners & Pilots Association

AMSL above mean sea level

ATC Air Traffic Control

ATCO Air Traffic Control Officer

ATIS Automatic Terminal Information System

ATZ Aerodrome Traffic Zone

Avgas Aviation fuel for piston engines

CAA Civil Aviation Authority

C of A Certificate of Airworthiness - necessary examination and documentation to allow flight of an aircraft

Chapter 11 company defence against creditors (similar to administration in UK)

Check "A" first check of an aircraft before each flight – a "walkaround"

EASA European Union Aviation Safety Agency

FIR Flight Information Region

FL80 Flight Level 8000 feet (measured against a standard pressure setting)

FREDA Check a regular check of Fuel, Radio, Engine, Direction, Altitude.

GAR General Aviation Report

Garmin manufacturer of GPS equipment

Glide Slope the indicated correct path to descend when using ILS

GPS Global Positioning System

ICAO International Civil Aviation Organisation

ICAO 4 letter codes first two letters identify country, second two indicate airport e.g. EG - UK; FA - South Africa; FQ – Mozambique; FV – Zimbabwe; FW – Malawi; HE – Egypt; HK – Kenya; HS – Sudan; HT – Tanzania; LF – France, LG – Greece, LI - Italy

IFR Instrument Flight Rules

ILS Instrument Landing System

IMC Instrument Meteorological Conditions – a rating to allow flight in non-VFR conditions

IR/R new name for the IMC

JET A-1 kerosene used to power jet and turbine aircraft

JNB airline nomenclature for Johannesburg Airport

Knots or Kts speed in nautical miles per hour

METARs Meteorological Actual Reports – the weather now

MOGAS normal petrol which can sometimes be used in an aero engine

Nav/Comm aircraft transceiver that also includes navigation equipment to interpret VOR and ILS signals

NM or Nautical Mile equivalent to 1.15 statute miles

PLB Personal Locator Beacon

PLOG pilot's log of planned headings, distances, timings

SAFA Safety Assessment of Foreign Aircraft

Semi-Circular rule approved flight levels dependant on headings

SkyEcho 2 a device that passes GPS data and warnings of ADS-B signals from nearby aircraft to SkyDemon

SkyDemon flight-planning and navigation system (and much more) that can run on phones or iPads/Androids

TAFs Terminal Area Forecasts for weather

TBO Time Before Overhaul – hours before must be replaced or maintained to acceptable tolerances

TMA terminal area airspace

True Air Speed speed of an aircraft through the air mass it is travelling in (adjusted for density)

VFR Visual Flight Rules

VOR VHF Omnidirectional Range – a beacon showing radials (directions from beacon in magnetic degrees)

What3Words a precise navigation system that identifies every 3 metres square of the world with a unique three-word reference

Zulu Sierra first letters of a South African aircraft registration

Printed in Great Britain
by Amazon